I0747779

Watermelon Days

Judy Turner

Watermelon Days

Watermelon Days
ISBN 978 1 76109 487 3
Copyright © text Judy Turner 2023
Cover image: Alexa from Pixabay

First published 2023 by
GINNINDERRA PRESS
PO Box 3461 Port Adelaide 5015
www.ginninderrapress.com.au

Contents

Wisteria

I pushed open the wrought-iron gate, remembering the countless times I'd done so as both child and adult. Each time I came home. Mum was always there, waiting; turning from whatever she was doing to ask about my day.

I followed the concrete path towards the house. That old sandstone house, its solid form crouched amidst the rambling gardens and ordered close-cut lawns. Mum's hydrangeas sat decked in frills of blue. She used to shelter them with two beach umbrellas on hot summer days. Mum loved those blue hydrangeas, and the vases inside the house were full of them each Christmas and January.

The cool green tiles of the front porch led me to the door with its cut-glass inserts. I pressed the bell and waited. No answer. I pushed it again, listening to the familiar chime echoing down the hall. No one home.

I headed back across the tiles and wandered around the side of the house to the backyard, noticing the cracks and fissures in the concrete path. Adelaide was notorious for its restless moving soil, cracking walls and paths.

It was dry and hot after London, the sky a cloudless blue. The blistering air scorched my nostrils as I inhaled. *And the light* – the glare of that Australian sunlight! My jet-lagged eyes were glad I'd remembered my sunglasses. I squared my shoulders. I was home in an Adelaide summer after four years away, and Adelaide summers were no place for hydrangeas.

The wisteria rambling over the back veranda had finished blooming, and I noticed it hadn't had the usual early summer prune. Dad often threatened to cut back the wisteria, but Mum wouldn't let him anywhere near it. She lovingly pruned it in summer and winter to ensure maximum cascades of purple blooms in spring.

Dad had protested when Mum brought it home from the nursery. He quoted from the gardening books: 'This plant is extremely vigorous and may become rampant…' 'displaying a most adventurous character…'

Mum stood with her hands on her hips, laughing, and I thought at that moment Dad could have been describing her. She turned, headed straight outside, dug a hole and planted the wisteria.

'Unruly nuisance of a plant,' Dad muttered, 'needs to be kept under control, like women and children.'

Dad was in charge of the lawns and Mum was the maestro of the gardens. Dad kept his lawns trimmed and orderly, while Mum's gardens were as flamboyant as her personality and the wisteria was a prime example as it traipsed unchecked up the patio posts and across the roof of the back veranda and house.

The rear door was locked, and I stood in the cool shade of the wisteria-covered veranda for a moment, my eyes sweeping around the backyard. Rediscovering the special places that were mine to go to as a child when I wanted to get away from Mum and Dad's fights, my sister's silly games or just life in general. The hollow at the side of the house between two tall shrubs was my favourite. The wisteria had overtaken the shrubs from above, leaving a perfect secret space for me to hide and play with my Matchbox cars or Star Wars figures, or simply daydream for an hour or two.

My present daydreams were interrupted by the sound of my phone.

'Harry, where are you? Are you in Adelaide yet?' My sister's voice held a note of panic.

'Hi, Gail. Yes, I'm at the house. Where is everyone?'

'At the Royal Adelaide. We had to call the ambulance during the night. Mum is much worse. She's asking for you.' Her words crackled with emotion. 'Do you want me to come and get you, Harry? The doctors say she hasn't got long.'

'I have a rental car. I'll be right there.'

Nothing can prepare you for the loss of a loved one. I was shocked by what remained of my mother after a year of cancer, of hideous surgery and chemo. All that lingered was a bundle of bones held together by translucent skin. She was lucid enough to recognise me at first as I bent and kissed her grey cheek.

She clutched at my arm. 'Harry, you came,' she said with a long sigh, and then immediately asked, 'How are you, son?'

Shortly after, I convinced Gail and Dad to go home for a shower and a rest, as they had been at the hospital all night. I sat, holding my mother's hand, remembering her as a young woman. Her smile, her palm on my forehead as she kissed me goodnight. Her crazy, impulsive ways. 'Let's go for a swim, kids', she would cry as we ate our cornflakes on warm summer mornings. And we would dash off to Glenelg beach, leaving dirty breakfast dishes on the table and toast crumbs on the floor.

Her indifference to housekeeping annoyed the life out of Dad, who liked an orderly household with everything in its place. 'Go home and live with your tidy mother if you don't like it,' Mum would yell at him. He never did, of course, and they were together in their ambivalent disharmony for fifty-four years of marriage.

When Mum died late that night, Dad put his head in his hands and sobbed in uncontrolled grief. Gail looked at me and raised her eyebrows as we hovered next to Dad's shuddering shoulders. Neither of us knew how to console him, both so astonished at this uncharacteristic display of raw emotion from our father. The following morning, we helped him clean up the house, ready for the funeral and wake.

One summer later, I returned home to see Dad. I paused a moment before opening the wrought-iron gate, recalling the terrible sadness of my last visit and my mother's death. The hydrangeas drooped in the heat and were pruned to about half their previous size.

I found Dad sitting on the back veranda. I sat down beside him, throwing my jacket across a nearby chair as I puffed out my cheeks and pulled the collar of my shirt away from my sweating neck.

Dad looked at me. 'Come inside,' he said. 'It's too hot out here on the veranda now the wisteria's gone.'

A Trivial Pursuit

Audrey and Joan wandered down the long narrow corridor of the cruise ship looking for cabin Aloha302. They passed many seemingly lost people wandering around on a similar mission. Finally, there it was, A302, their names tagged on the door. Their steward greeted them with a big smile and introduced herself as *Mary from the Philippines.*

Later that day, Audrey was a bit unsettled when she saw their table waiter's name tag: *Jesus. The Philippines.*

'I'm not sure how much fun we can have with Mary and Jesus watching over us,' she remarked as they settled into the comfortable chairs of the music lounge after dinner.

A waiter named *Matthew from India* came and took their drink order.

'Looks like the Twelve Apostles may be on board the ship as well,' whispered Joan.

They were on the *Sunset Princess* cruising twenty-seven days to Los Angeles, followed by five nights in Hollywood before their Qantas flight back to Sydney.

When Audrey saw the ad for the last minute, bargain cruise fares, she phoned Joan and suggested they book a special holiday to celebrate their seventieth birthdays. 'Let's go play the merry widows and we can see Hollywood at last.'

They had been friends since schooldays in their sprawling country town. When they were girls, they swept off together to the magic of Hollywood every Saturday afternoon. As the lights dimmed, they embraced the expectant dark and escaped from the everyday predictability that was their rural town's life.

For sixpence, they had enjoyed cartoons, a newsreel, the weekly serial and two full-length movies. Each Saturday, they held their breath as the hero of the serial hung by a fingernail until the next exciting episode. They laughed at the capers of Abbott and Costello, Danny Kaye, Jerry Lewis and Dean Martin, and gasped at the adventures of Tarzan, Superman, and the Lone Ranger. They thundered their feet on the wooden floor and cheered loudly as the cavalry charged in to kill off yet another tribe of hostile Indians.

Eventually, they left behind the boisterous adventures of the Saturday arvo matinees and graduated to the evening screenings of musicals and romances. The silver screen presented them with weekly dreams and hopes. However, they were only dreams and nothing but blind hope really for the daughters of the rural working class. Three years of high school was the best education they could expect – and then a job in a shop or something similar until they found a bloke to marry.

As teenagers, they'd both lusted after Richard Chalmers, one of the local grazier's sons. Richard was at primary school with them but was despatched to boarding school in Sydney for his high school education. That meant they only had the opportunity to bat their eyelashes at him during school holidays. They made sure they ran into him wherever possible – at church on Sundays, at the pictures, or swimming down at the weir. One Saturday, Richard put a Jaffa down the back of Joan's dress just as Rock Hudson and Doris Day finally kissed in *Pillow Talk*. Joan thought about that a lot afterwards.

It was Patricia Bonnell, however, who snatched up Richard Chalmers. She was the daughter of the other rich grazier in the district. Funny how money attracts money. It was a waste, actually, as Patricia cleared out with one of Richard's rich Sydney friends after only two years of marriage. By then, Audrey and Joan were both well and truly settled.

They married hard-working, decent men – a butcher and a mechanic. Both women felt they did all right for themselves. They raised their children and lived reasonably contented lives until the two husbands upped and died earlier in the year, Tom first with lung cancer and then Bill from a heart attack.

Audrey sipped her drink and gave their fellow passengers the once-over. 'The blokes onboard all seem to be candidates for surgical stockings.'

Joan laughed. 'And there are a few really tragic comb-overs. I wonder how they manage out on a windy deck.'

'I don't feel as ancient as most of these old codgers. Do you?'

'No way,' said Joan.

They settled back and watched couples foxtrotting around the dance floor. An older woman danced by in the arms of a young man. She had a fixed, surprised look on her face.

'She's found a toy boy,' muttered Audrey.

'Definitely had some work done on her face,' said Joan. 'Did you see where her eyebrows were? Nearly up at her hairline.'

'Gawd, cop the outfit. Talk about mutton dressed as lamb! Doesn't she have a mirror? Or a friend?'

'She looks a bit familiar.' Joan peered after the couple.

The two friends turned to each other. 'It couldn't be!'

'Looks a bit like her!'

'I'm gonna find out.' Audrey heaved herself to her feet and headed across the dance floor.

Joan hesitated for just a moment before she leapt up and hurried after her.

'Was your maiden name Patricia Bonnell by any chance?' Audrey ventured.

'Who are you?' The frozen face squinted up at the two women.

'Audrey and Joan – I think we went to school together – St Bernard's at...'

'Oh! Audrey and...?'

'Joan!'

The band started playing 'Moon River'.

Patricia turned to her toy boy and gave him a tight smile, 'Darling, it's our song.'

He took her hand, and they swept off in a jazz waltz; leaving Audrey and Joan standing open-mouthed on the edge of the dance floor.

That night, Joan peered at her wrinkled face as she rubbed in the bio-oil. Seventy years of sun, laughter and hard work had left their mark. It didn't seem so long ago that she was a teenager lusting after Richard Chalmers and hating Patricia Bonnell for pinching him. She'd seen Richard in Woolies just before they left. He'd tipped his hat and said good morning. He'd never remarried.

'Don't be ridiculous,' she muttered to herself.

Mary had a hard time convincing Audrey and Joan they didn't have to make their beds each morning.

'I've made my bed every morning for seventy years. Can't stop now,' said Audrey.

Mary loved them. In fact, all the staff on the ship soon knew and loved Audrey and Joan. The two friends went out of their way to be friendly and take an interest in the comings and goings of the crew. The women were horrified at the length of time staff worked onboard away from home. Mary shyly showed them a photo of her family and Joan had to know all their names, their ages and everything about them. Mary sometimes put an extra chocolate on their pillows.

Audrey was resolute that they waste not one moment on their cruise. She was determined to get full value for their hard-earned money. Every port was an adventure. They scattered their laughter, sense of wonder and exuberance right across the Pacific. Every evening, they examined the onboard activities for the next day and ticked off all the things they wanted to do. They played five hundred and bingo, learnt napkin-folding, card making, quilling and beading, and went to every lecture. They were always first in the theatre for the evening shows. They loved the glitz and glamour of the big musical shows.

They even tried the stretch class in the gym one morning. One of Audrey's daughters had convinced her mother to buy a special tracksuit for the trip. It was deep blue with bright fluoro lime-green and purple inserts.

Audrey had rubbed her hands over her multicoloured Lycra-clad hips as she stood in the Target change room. 'I don't know, Tracey. I'm not exactly Jane Fonda.'

'Mum, it looks good. It will be very handy for the cruise. *And it's on sale! 30% off!*

They found sneakers to match.

The morning Audrey and Joan set out for the gym on the ship, Joan wore just an old loose pair of slacks and T-shirt, but Audrey really looked the part in her new outfit. Neither woman had ever been near a gym. Joan walked each morning. Longer and harder since Bill had died of his heart attack. The most exercise Audrey had over the past forty years was giving Tom and the kids the rounds of the kitchen.

Yaakov, a muscular young man from Ukraine, ran the stretch class. He was very serious and barked abrupt, stern instructions at the group. 'Lay on floor. Now, straight up leg please!'

Audrey and Joan watched the others and tried not to giggle as they raised their legs into the air. The next instruction proved Audrey's undoing.

'Roll up yourself,' commanded Yaakov.

Audrey collapsed into uncontrollable laughter and lay like a helpless, multicoloured Christmas beetle on her back.

Yaakov gave a snort and growled, 'Serious face in stretch class please.'

After that, Joan decided that a few laps around the deck each day would be a suitable airing for Audrey's tracksuit.

Their favourite pastime on board ship was the very popular daily trivia contest. At home, they played weekly at the pub and their team had won the trophy for the past four years. On the ship, they teamed up with Shirley and Kevin, a couple from Melbourne who shared their dining table. Shirley and Kevin had spent most of their retirement cruising, 'spending the kids' inheritance,' and were now Elite passengers. They took a shine to Audrey and Joan and took delight in showing them 'the ropes' around the ship. Shirley and Kevin loved trivial pursuit and were shrewd enough to see what an asset Audrey and Joan were to their team. The only fly in the ointment was that Patricia and her toy boy had a rather impressive group of six.

'That toy boy is not as dim as he looks,' muttered Audrey one day as they lost for the second time in a row.

There was a trophy at the end of the cruise for the team with the highest total score, and, so far, Patricia's group was ahead by two points. Audrey and her team were determined to win.

As they drew closer to Los Angeles, they abandoned bingo and all their craft activities. They spent any spare time in the library. Shirley and Kevin used their free internet access to print out pages of trivial pursuit questions and answers. It was a serious challenge.

Most of the staff knew of the contest and called out good wishes to Audrey and Joan as they made their way for the finals of the Trivial Pursuit Challenge in the crowded Wheelhouse Lounge. Patricia and her toy boy had made themselves unpopular with both crew and passengers by their arrogant, snobbish behaviour and everyone was rooting for the Audrey team.

Patricia's team won by one point.

One of the other team leaders spotted the toy boy with his iPad under the table.

'We had a blind hope of winning against that,' said Audrey.

'We'll report him for cheating,' said Kevin.

'No,' said Audrey. 'If they have to cheat to win, that's their loss. Anyway, we got two bottles of champagne – much better than a tinny trophy!'

'Such is life,' said Joan. 'Let's pop a bottle and celebrate. At least we can have a good laugh without cracking our faces. And *tomorrow* we'll be in Hollywood.'

The Fish

I walk the dusty, winding road to the village. There is only a small bar fridge in the villa where John and I have stayed now for four days, so I shop each morning for our daily needs.

Today is market day and I wander amongst the noise and bustle of the market stalls, observing the exuberance of the vendors as they banter with discerning customers. Italians are such animated conversationalists; I love to watch their faces as they bargain and barter. And the hands! Could any Italians converse without using their hands?

No one hurries, and I learn from the shoppers as they examine and choose each item with meticulous care. Most pause and smile when they hear my terrible attempts at their language. I move from stall to stall, breathing in the scents of basil, oregano and thyme and admire the freshness of neatly stacked produce.

A wrinkled, grey-haired woman, in a black dress, crumpled stockings and feet clad in purple plastic crocs, tries to convince me to buy her fish. She peppers me with a rapid-fire of incomprehensible Italian, and then beams, gives an extravagant gesture with both hands, and declares *'Pesce…freschissimoo! Bello, bello!'*

I carry home the 'very fresh, beautiful fish', some lemons, sweet red tomatoes, salad greens, and crusty bread.

Later, as I wash and dry the fish, I remember nineteen-year-old Sally preparing the whole snapper for her father's fiftieth birthday. Her long blonde hair fell curtain-like over her face as she worked, her entire body intent on the task.

'I want to cook a special dinner for Dad,' she had earlier declared. 'It has to be fish, of course. And snapper – it must be snapper!'

I drove her to the fish market, where she patiently inspected each stall, smiling and chatting with the fishmongers until she found the freshest and best fish. A whole beautiful snapper, John's favourite fish. She baked it with butter, lemon and herbs and it was delicious.

A tiny snapper, barely legal size, was the first fish Sally ever caught. She was five years old and squealed with excitement as her father helped her pull it into the boat. She was the only one to catch a fish on that salty summer day, and her two older brothers were just a little jealous. John threw the fish on the barbecue with the sausages. Sally gave us each a small spoonful of her prize to taste. She was such a generous, gracious little girl.

Her generosity later led to trouble. It was her first semester at university. John had encouraged the boys into trade apprenticeships, but he had been very proud when Sally decided to go to uni.

'A university education, eh? Like your mother.'

'Plumbers earn a lot more than teachers, Dad,' Sally laughed.

She moved away from home to the city into a group house. She met Greg, a homeless boy, and offered him a mattress on the floor of her room to tide him over. He soon moved into her bed, and they shared everything, including the drugs he loved so much.

What happened to our lovely daughter? What made her do what she did? Why didn't we help her more?

Our beautiful, intelligent, gregarious Sally. The mood swings, the poor exam results – all should have been warning signs. We kept hoping it would pass, and I kept praying Greg would disappear. He eventually did, but so did our Sally.

Things got pretty rocky in our marriage after that. John was angry and confused. I was frozen with shock and grief. I moved into Sally's old room because I couldn't sleep. The sleeping pills the doctor prescribed did not work. The antidepressants made me feel worse, and I only took them for two days before flushing the lot down the toilet. I lay on the bed for a week staring at the ceiling, wondering where we went wrong. What more should we have done?

Both the boys phoned and left messages from time to time. I knew

I should ring them back, but couldn't. They had both moved away. Made lives for themselves. Sensible boys, with good jobs and relationships. I told myself they were okay. But I had thought that about Sally. I should phone them. Tomorrow.

John appeared in the doorway from time to time, shifting from one foot to the other and looking anxious. He flew my mother down from Brisbane. I was furious, but I guess he was desperate. Mum scrubbed the house, rearranged things in every cupboard, filled the freezer with containers of food and then went home.

Before she left, she came and stood by my bed and sniffed. 'Jennifer, you know you are not the only person in the world to suffer a loss. You have a husband and two sons to consider beside yourself. It's time you got up and returned to work.'

Of course, she was right as usual.

People skirted around me at work. No one knew what to say. How to handle the manic look in my eyes. The kids in my class were quiet and well behaved for the first few days, and then I was thankful when they became boisterous and naughty again. It was the normality of those kids and my work that kept me upright. I dreaded the thought of school holidays.

I took up yoga, tried acupuncture to help me sleep, and started an Italian language course. Nothing worked.

One counsellor told me I must cry. 'Crying is part of the journey to unravel the intricate knot of grief,' she said.

I stared at her, listening to her stupid platitudes. What did she know about grief? Had she experienced it first-hand? She was young and attractive. Probably had a yuppie boyfriend and a yuppie lifestyle and never shed a tear in her life. I couldn't cry.

John left. He had an affair. Where did he meet her? When? I wondered about the twenty-nine years of smug complacency on my part. I believed we had a good marriage, but I had been wrong about a lot of things. I wasn't angry with him. I was no longer capable of feeling anger.

Two months later, he walked back through the door and begged me to take him back. I sat there numb. Nothing touched me any more. I just sat there clutching my wine glass, looking at him.

'I've been such an idiot, Jen. Please forgive me. It was Sally…the complete bloody tragedy. I didn't know what I was doing. I've been such a fool.'

'Yes,' I said. I meant yes, he'd been a fool, but, of course, he thought I meant yes, I'd take him back.

'Thanks, Jen.' He took a glass from the cupboard and moved across to the sink. 'Tap's dripping. Needs a new washer. Guess my coming back will save you having to get a plumber.'

'Yes,' I said.

He suggested we go to the villa in Italy to celebrate our thirtieth wedding anniversary. A strange proposition from an Aussie plumber who loved fishing. On the other hand, the boat had sat unused in the carport now for many months. I realised the Italian thing was for me. Things hadn't been that great since he moved back. We skirted around each other, sashaying through each day in a polite little well-mannered square dance.

The tiny villa is lovely. It is quiet here in early spring; the main thrust of tourists is yet to arrive. A fresh greenness on the grapevines unfurls before our eyes. The car has sat in the drive since we pulled up four days ago. We agreed to leave the sightseeing for a while, both of us content to settle in slowly.

I sit on the terrace each morning with my coffee and a book, often reading the same page repeatedly. Gazing out over the fields of Tuscany, I breathe in the warm morning sun and hope for healing. Each day, I pray for healing.

John takes off on long walks, roaming the hills from town to town alone. When I ask what he does there, he tells me he just sits in the piazzas with the other old men.

Yesterday, he arrived back grinning, a light in his eyes I hadn't seen for a long time, the words tumbling out: 'The village I found today had this cluttered little hardware shop, run by a tiny gnome of a bloke in a leather apron. He had more stock than Bunnings crammed into two small rooms. And in the yard, you should see the slabs of marble, old carved wooden doors, fireplaces. All sorts of things! Bloody amazing!'

He sheepishly pulled a brass screw from his pocket. 'Felt I had to buy something. The door handle fitting in the second bedroom is missing a screw.' He headed off towards the kitchen. 'I wonder if there's a screwdriver somewhere. Or maybe a knife that'll do the job.'

I smiled as I listened to him opening and slamming drawers. A man on a mission.

The smells of fish, lemon and butter rise with the steam when I peel back the foil. The opaque eye of the fish gives me a dead milky stare as I carry the dish to the table.

'Ah,' says John, 'looks delicious. Wonder what it is? Must be freshwater. Looks a bit like a perch of some sort.'

He is good at serving fish, good at gently lifting the flesh away from the bones. I watch his strong, capable hands take up the servers, as I have watched his hands so many times haul fish into the boat. That boat! His pride and the children's excitement the night he towed it home.

'Now we can go fishing,' he declared as the children danced around him.

'When, Dad, when?'

'As soon as you all know how to look after these.' He reached into the boat and produced three fishing rods. 'Before we even go out in the boat, you have to learn about knots. The first thing a good fisherman learns is how to tie a secure knot. If you lose a hook, you have to fix your own rig. We'll have a lesson on knots after dinner tonight.'

He showed such patience as he taught the children how to unravel and re-rig their lines. I remember smiling, their bodies bent over lines and hooks as they practised. The Blood Knot, rhe Half-blood Knot. But it was John's favourite knot that thrilled them the most…

John places a serving of fish on each of our plates. I bite into a small piece. It has an odd, peculiar texture, and a strange flavour. I am shocked by the tears that roll down my face. I taste their salt on my lips. 'Do you remember her first fish?' I whisper.

John comes around the table and kneels beside me, taking my hand. 'Jen, don't.'

We both saw the brutal mark that unforgiving rope made on our daughter's beautiful neck. We both saw the too-perfect knot she tied in the rope that day. The knot John so carefully taught the children long ago.

'Both strong and easy to tie,' he told them. 'Look closely now,' he said, and the three of them leant in towards him and then repeatedly practised until they got it right. The Hangman's Knot.

John's arms are around my body now. We are both crying, the first real tears we have shed together.

'I miss her so much,' he says softly.

'I'm sorry about the fish,' I sniff.

John rises and scrapes the plates into the bin. 'Will I make toast? There's some cheese and, oh, those great tomatoes you bought.'

I nod, blow my nose, and take a gulp of wine. John moves around the kitchen, preparing food. Capable. Strong. Present.

I take a deep breath. 'Should we drive to Sienna tomorrow? Have lunch and do a little sightseeing? Perhaps buy some nice veal for scaloppini?'

Mayonnaise and Mayhem

'*Lamborghini*! We'll call her *Lamb*orghini!' Anna cried when our pet sheep, Barbarella, produced her first lamb.

'Anna, remember what Steve said about never naming farm animals.'

'But, Mark, *you know* we'll never eat her.'

We moved from the city two years ago to our lovely home, with its wide verandas and views over thirty acres of fields, rolling hills and forest. Two magnificent gum trees stood as sentinels in the side field. Our neighbour Steve told us these trees were probably over a hundred-years-old. That morning I'd watched a fierce red sun rise slowly over the horizon. Drought the past two years had parched the land. We were desperate for rain.

The heat rapidly intensified as the day progressed. I spotted smoke billowing in the distance and busied myself clearing the house gutters and downpipes, wondering if I should fill them with water. But the smoke was far away, and the Rural Fire Service website indicated no danger to our area.

From the start, we made sure we got involved in local affairs. We didn't want to be branded a couple of *blow-ins* from the city. Tonight, we were off to a fund-raising get-together at the Rural Hall. No doubt women in kitchens around the neighbourhood were cooking up a storm, and Anna was busy making a seriously large potato salad.

I heard Steve's horn tooting non-stop before I saw his truck screaming down our drive.

'Get out now,' he yelled. 'The wind's changed. The fire's heading straight for you.'

I ran inside. Anna stood at the kitchen bench, a jar of mayonnaise in her hand.

'Anna, we have to get out. The wind's changed.'

'But the recipe said it's important to put the mayonnaise on the potatoes while they're hot.'

'Anna, we have to go. I'll get the computer stuff and see to the animals You grab anything precious you want. I'll see you outside in *one minute.*'

She stood, still holding the jar of mayonnaise. 'Should I drive my car?'

'No, we should go together. *One minute, Anna! Quick!*'

I threw our laptops and external drives into a bag, leaving it at the back door as I ran out and whistled the dog.

I raced to the nearest paddock and opened the gate. Barbarella and Lamborghini grazed at the bottom of the hill. The dog, usually barking and boisterous at the prospect of rounding up the sheep, now whimpered and pressed against my leg.

We stood in a strangely surreal, amber light, aware of a distant, low, growling rumble. Fierce orange now coloured the sky on the horizon. The blistering wind strengthened, spewing forth ash and embers. Then a loud roaring sound, unlike anything I'd ever heard. *No time to help the poor sheep!* I turned and fled, flinging the chicken pen door open as I sprinted past.

Anna was running along the front veranda. 'Where's the cat?' she screamed. 'He was here a minute ago.'

Our cat, Pusseidon, was king of the house, treating Anna, myself and the dog with equal, tail-in-the-air disdain. Anna adored him.

I couldn't believe how quickly the savage orange fireball moved towards us, engorging itself with life from the earth, sucking oxygen from the air. The day became night as thick black smoke blocked the sun.

'We have to find the cat,' wailed Anna.

I could hardly breathe as I ran around the side of the house. *Where was that bloody cat?* Radiant heat from the approaching fire was horrendous. Embers rained down around us. I saw flames erupting from the treetops and spot fires crackled into ignition on dry paddock grass.

'Get in the car.' I yelled at Anna.

The dog didn't need to be told.

The wind blew debris and embers horizontally across the road and onto the windscreen as we headed for town. Thick smoke surrounded us and I was driving almost blind. A fire truck screamed out on our right. We followed its flashing lights through the smoky haze. It was then I realised we'd left the precious bags behind.

Late next day, we found the remains of our beloved cat in the pile of ash and rubble that was once our lovely home. The fire meticulously reaped a savage harvest: the house and contents, sheds, fences. Everything gone! One of our magnificent gum trees lay like a fallen warrior across the paddock. The other stood alongside, a blackened tombstone. The charred forest scarred the surrounding hills. Ghostly skeletons of a vanquished army. The chickens had vanished without a trace, but, by some miracle, Barbarella and Lamborghini survived.

Fishing for Blackfish

My heart thumped as I left the station on that first call-out after a year off work following the accident. A trail bike rider had phoned. Said he'd hit a tree, trying to avoid an old bloke lying unconscious across a track by the river. I hoped the ambos got there before me.

From the location, I figured the old bloke might be Charlie Moon. Dad and I used to see Charlie Moon fishing for blackfish from his little tinnie near the ruins of the jetty at the back of the river. Dad and I never *could* catch blackfish. We tried and tried, but never got the knack.

'It takes special *know-how* to be able to catch blackfish,' Dad said. 'Old Charlie Moon has it. I wish I knew his secret.'

Charlie had lived down by the river since the late 1940s. When he was younger, he used to do odd jobs for the Maguires and old Mr Maguire let him build a shack in a remote, uncleared part of the property. Dad told me that Charlie was a prisoner of war on the Thai/Burma Railway. My wife Robyn and I visited the site of that Death Railway years ago as we backpacked around Thailand. Robyn said it was the saddest place she'd ever been.

The ambos had Charlie on the stretcher when I arrived.

'Not good,' said Steve quietly as he closed the ambulance door. 'The kid's all right. Just a scrape and a bit of a shake-up. We'll take him in for a check. You okay, Jeff?'

Steve had been at my last call-out. A year ago. When the body on the stretcher was my eight-year-old son.

For months, I stayed home on the bed, staring at the ceiling, limbs too heavy to move. I couldn't stomach going out, watching people go about their daily business as though nothing had happened. Didn't they understand that the whole world had changed and the pulverising grief was unbearable? The police department organised counselling and compassionate leave, and then I took all my sick and long-service leave.

People deal with grief in different ways. My wife Robyn is a nurse. Robyn squared her shoulders and took on extra shifts. She's just skin and bones. I often hear her sobbing in the bathroom, but she gets up every morning and faces the day. We hardly talk these days.

Charlie died on the way to the hospital. Next morning, I trudged along the track towards the river, the track Charlie Moon walked for over seventy years. His wallet did not indicate any next of kin, so I headed down to his shack to investigate further.

It was clean and tidy inside. The meagre furnishings reflecting the Spartan existence of its owner, who had lived here in isolation since the end of the Second World War. The older people in town respected his need for privacy. Men like old Maguire knew something of the scars of war, understood how it might affect a man.

I found a wooden box in the wardrobe and discovered a yellowed birth certificate revealing Charlie's age to be ninety-three, his army discharge papers and two old photos. One photo was of a young soldier with a beautiful woman. The other, which was very creased and water damaged, was of the same woman holding a baby. I turned it over and read the faded, smudged writing on the back. 'Darling Charlie, what do you think of your wife and son? Love, Madge and John.'

What happened to Madge and John? Did Madge meet someone else while Charlie was away enduring the horrors of the POW camps? Did he carry that photo of his wife and son through the rain and mud and miseries of Hellfire Pass, only to come back to nothing? I shook my head as I looked around the old bare hut and thought of Charlie Moon's seventy years of seclusion there with no wife and son.

As a youngster, I saw Charlie pulling in those blackfish with such skill and questioned how anyone could retreat inside himself to such an extent. Now I understood, as I had no son to fish with either.

Closing the door, I gazed out through the trees towards the sunlight streaming down on the river and wondered if the old man found peace in this tranquil place? I used to feel sorry for old Charlie and his isolation, but it certainly was a beautiful, peaceful spot to live the life of his choice. Perhaps I had been wrong. Perhaps I could learn something from his strength and resilience in surviving the horrors of war and hardships on his return.

I strolled down and squatted by the old jetty, wondering if I would ever learn to catch blackfish. A fish jumped midstream. The water rippled and then stilled. 'Rest in peace, Charlie Moon,' I said.

As I headed back to town, I thought about the possibilities of tracking down the son John. But first I had to speak to Robyn.

Eleven Pairs of Sandshoes

A ten-day safari in Kenya, Africa! I couldn't believe my luck when my boss offered me the opportunity. A bonus of my work as a travel agent was the occasional offer to experience a tourist destination first-hand. And this trip was with Abercrombie and Kent, the crème de la crème of African safari travel companies.

Three weeks later, the eleven agents chosen gathered at Sydney airport, introducing ourselves, eyeing each other off. Ten women and one bloke. Lucky devil, he would get a single room. I wondered who my roommate might be, hoping it might be one of the quiet ones, and not the loudmouth woman holding court at the front. Why was there always one who had to have the limelight? The best seat in the bus? The best room?

We eventually arrived at Nairobi airport early evening and discovered that not one piece of our luggage had arrived with us. The airport staff shrugged. It was still in Johannesburg? Or maybe in Sydney? No one was sure. They would investigate and try to get it to us sometime. But it wouldn't be for a while, as the next flight from Johannesburg was in three days.

Our Abercrombie and Kent guide introduced herself as Serena. She was a tall, slender, ebony-skinned woman with a toothpaste-ad smile, her long hair tied back in a multitude of beaded braids. She suggested we enjoy a meal and a good night's sleep at our Nairobi hotel and promised to take us shopping for emergency clothing the following morning.

Eleven toothbrushes and tubes of toothpaste waited for us at the hotel and I learnt I was sharing with Vanessa from New Zealand. Vanessa and I bonded that night as we washed our panties in the bathroom and she laughed about her husband missing out on her sleeping naked for the first time in her life.

The following day, we visited a local department store for spare undies and pyjamas. Our loudmouth member declared she must also visit the cosmetic counter. Then, we were off to a safari outfit shop where Serena suggested we each buy three T-shirts, a pair of shorts, a hat and a sweatshirt. There was only one cubicle for trying on our purchases, and the local staff laughed at our antics as we ducked in and out, choosing our gear.

'Don't get a red T-shirt,' one advised, 'you'll frighten the lions.'

The next stop was the shoe shop. The young black shop assistant's eyes popped when we trooped in and demanded eleven pairs of sandshoes. He carefully measured our feet, wrote a list and dashed out the door, fiddling with the lock as he departed.

Vanessa went and tried the door. 'He's locked us in,' she cried.

'Making sure he doesn't lose the best sale he's ever likely to have,' I said.

Soon he was back, accompanied by two young black men, each bearing a pile of shoeboxes.

Nothing like losing your luggage for a bit of bonding and equilibrium! We boarded our two safari vans and set off from Nairobi each clad in khaki shorts and matching sandshoes – the colours of the T-shirts, the only signs of individuality.

Our loudmouth member complained bitterly about the special safari outfit lost in her luggage. Serena told us all our bags had been located in Johannesburg and should be on the next flight in three days.

Africa! The stress and traumas of work and home became just a dim memory. The scenery, the animals, the people were all amazing. I felt calm and grounded in this wonderful land, my sandshoes plodding softly on the Kenyan soil.

Even our loudmouth was quiet the next morning as we sat in the safari vans, watching two cheetahs hunt down their prey as the dawn light crept above the thorn trees. A tower of giraffes loped gracefully past. Our two nights and one full day in Samburu Game Reserve were unforgettable and the range of animals beyond my expectations. Elephants, zebra, lion, leopard, baboon and more.

But the most amazing experience of all occurred as we headed back to the lodge near dusk. We encountered a pride of lions padding along the track led by a huge black-maned male. Two juveniles decided to climb a large acacia tree and sat along the branches. Three other juveniles joined them, and the females of the pride plonked themselves down in the dust of the trail with an air of resigned maternal patience. The black-maned alpha male stood looking at this for a few moments and then gave a deafening roar. The lionesses rose, the juveniles came down from the tree, and the whole pride padded off down the trail, leaving us all breathless with wonder.

On the fourth day, we travelled south to Tree Tops Safari Lodge in Aberdare National Park. We were informed that this was where Princess Elizabeth was staying when her father died in 1952. 'She went to bed a princess and woke up a queen,' Serena said, and then went on to tell us that Tree Tops had a thousand-watt artificial moon to illuminate the animals at the waterhole during darkness and management kept noise at low decibels because of some animals' hearing sensitivity. This included prohibiting any hard-soled shoes. We all looked down at our sandshoe-clad feet and laughed.

Tree Tops Lodge was special. I stayed up all night, fascinated by the spectacle of animals coming and going from the salt-licks to the waterhole.

The waiter brought me a hot chocolate. 'You like the animals,' he stated.

I nodded, my hands clasped around the mug.

'They are life,' he said.

I have never experienced such peace as I did that night, watching those animals.

Our luggage arrived late on the fifth day of our safari, on the night before we were due to fly to the Maasai Mara Reserve. We were told we could only take an overnight bag on the small aircraft and I looked through the suitcase full of stuff I really didn't need.

The next morning, most of us still wore our khaki shorts and sand-shoes. Except for the one lady in a fancy safari suit.

Looking For Lunch

Nancy put down her coffee and opened the letter. Electricity account, twice the amount of the previous one. She did a mental rejig of her budget, wondering how her single pension could stretch to pay the mounting bills.

Last week after Bill's funeral, she'd trudged along the beach to the rocks below the headland. An incoming tide, a dangerous time at that spot, but something drew her there. She watched the swell of the sea; the waves crashing on the black rocks. Sucking back, exploding in once again. Pounding, eroding. The seagulls wheeling behind, screaming. She lifted her arms and screamed with them. Screamed for all the years life had thrashed her with one storm surge after another. But the rocks endured. Wrinkled and scarred, but they endured. And so would she.

A car pulled up in front of the house. Battered door, plastic taped over one window. A tall, thin figure emerged from the driver's side and a small girl from the back.

Nancy remembered the events leading up to her son's departure twelve years ago. Wave after wave of tension between stepson and stepfather building and ebbing, until it finally exploded in an eruption of violence, shouting and blows. Bill lying on the floor, bleeding, yelling, 'Get out of my house, you bloody no-hoper. Get out and never come back.'

Nancy walked down the path to meet her visitors. They stopped a foot or so apart, mother and son. And the child, staring, clinging to Ben's leg.

'The prodigal son returns,' he said. 'This is Skye, your granddaughter.'

He gave the girl a gentle shove, and she moved forward and threw her thin arms around her grandmother's thighs.

Nancy placed her hand on the brown head. 'Well,' she said with a long outward breath. 'Well! I don't have a fatted calf, but there is some soup. Want to come in for lunch?' But she realised he was there looking for more than just lunch after twelve years.

Ben cleared his throat. 'Mum, a mate has found me a job in Western Australia. Good money. I only need a few months to earn enough to get back on my feet. I can't take a four-year-old with me. Skye's mother pissed off a year ago. I don't have a clue where she is. Skye's a good kid, Mum. She'll be no trouble. I'll send you money as soon as I get settled.'

Nancy heard the desperation in her son's voice, saw the tremor of his hands, the undernourished body and pallid skin.

She shook her head. 'The poor child has only just met me. How can you leave her with a complete stranger?'

'Time for you both to get to know each.'

'How did you know to come *now*?'

'Uncle Stan found me in Sydney and told me Bill died. A mate lent me his car to drive down. Can we stay a couple of days *please*, Mum? You and Skye can see if you get along. Then *you* decide.'

But he was gone the next morning, along with fifty dollars from her purse, and he left no contact number.

Skye cried for her father that night. Nancy went to her and discovered the wet sheets.

Things settled down over the following weeks. Nancy and the child established a routine of sorts in the small coastal town, although the nights sometimes betrayed Skye's insecurity with wet beds and nightmares.

No money arrived from Ben. A friend suggested Nancy should go to Centrelink for some kind of carer's assistance.

'And have child welfare nosing around? No thanks!'

'They may be able to help you, Nancy,' Rita insisted.

'Those bastards didn't help me last time I asked for help. No thanks!'

Months passed with still no word from Ben. Most days, Nancy and Skye walked to the beach, roamed along the shore and explored the rock pools. Soon, the water would be warm enough and she could teach the child to swim.

The morning sunshine warmed Nancy as she lay back on the sand, her body weary from the nights of broken sleep. She closed her eyes, listening to the girl chatting away to her seaweed friends in an imaginary game.

Nancy woke to find Skye gone. Her eyes swept up and down the beach and then spotted the tiny figure amongst the rocks under the headland. She puffed her way along the sand.

'Skye, Skye,' she cried when she reached the child beside the rock pool. 'You must never come here without me. I told you that!' She was still breathless from the run from the beach. Her voice shook with anger at herself for falling asleep and anxiety for the child's safety.

Skye backed away. She threw one arm up in front of her face, panic in her voice. 'I just came to see the crab.'

The instinctive defence reflex from the girl shocked Nancy. She had done it herself so many times.

With a soft moan, she bent and wrapped her arms around the trembling, thin little body. 'It's okay, bub. It's okay. But next time you must wake me. You know how the waves can break over the rocks. They could come in and sweep you away.'

'I knew not to go near the edge,' Skye sniffed.

Nancy looked at the child's wide brown eyes and remembered Ben's eyes at that age as they snatched him from her.

How many nights had he cried out for her? All her past mistakes, all those poor decisions...

It *must not* happen again.

The ocean swelled and ebbed, benign and peaceful for now. Waves splashed against the glistening black rocks. A solitary gull whirled above the sea, graceful, silent.

Nancy took Skye's hand. 'Come on, let's go home, and see what we can find for lunch.'

Eucalyptus Oil

When I was young, my father would sprinkle drops of eucalyptus oil onto a spoonful of sugar and give it to me whenever I had a cold. I loved it! It wasn't until I was an adult that I learnt it was poisonous. However, I survived Dad's eucalyptus cold remedy and still have a love affair with the smell and taste of eucalyptus to this day.

The packer lifted the bottle and grinned. 'This is the first one of these I've packed!'

I had decided that a big bottle of eucalyptus oil (along with three large jars of Vegemite) should be amongst our personal effects to go by sea freight when we travelled to Ottawa, Canada, to live for a year in 1985.

Earlier, when we announced the plans to our four sons, we received mixed reactions: Peter (ten) and Robert (twelve) were enraptured by the promised stop at Disneyland on the way. Stephen (fifteen) expressed reservations about leaving his friends and starting in a strange school; but then warmed to the thoughts of skiing, camping, and visiting the national parks throughout North America. Jeffrey (sixteen) stated that he was not going and stormed off to his room, slammed the door, threw things around and then kicked out at his wardrobe door, making a hole in it. Ray went off to have a long talk with him. Nothing more was said. Ray repaired the hole that next weekend and we all knew Jeff was coming.

The boys couldn't believe their luck as we settled into business class on the Qantas flight on our first leg from Sydney to Tahiti. They thought they were in heaven. As much Coke as they could drink *and* movies *and* fancy food – all at the press of a button!

'It's like being hit in the face with a warm, wet towel!' Rob remarked accurately as we emerged from the plane in Papeete.

The hot fug of moist air that greeted us was indeed a complete contrast to the frosty spring dawn we had left behind in Canberra that morning.

After overnight in Papeete, we caught the ferry to the island of Moorea for a two-night stay.

The huge Tahitian guy in charge of the water sports laughed as he peered across the counter at Jeffrey's size thirteen feet. 'You don't need flippers, man. You have your own!'

I understand why the *Bounty* sailors fell in love with Tahiti. We snorkelled in the blue lagoon, lay on the white coral sand, and enjoyed the tropical warmth. However, Ray and I kept scanning the mounting food bill. Feeding four hungry sons was expensive in French Polynesia. 'Save up for the next business class leg. Knock another coconut from the tree,' we said.

The boys managed a hearty meal before nodding off on our eight-hour flight to Los Angeles.

A young Amazonian black woman shanghaied us as we emerged blinking from the LA airport terminal. 'You guys need a transfer to Disneyland,' she stated as she hurled our luggage into the back of her beat-up van.

Before we knew it, we were whizzing around the complex overpasses and hurtling down the freeway towards Anaheim.

Four chairs flew off a truck in front of us, and we all took a sharp intake of breath as our *warrior-driver* spun the steering wheel with one hand, whipping our van into another lane. Her other hand reached for the radio mike to report the carnage as vehicles swerved and braked to avoid the chairs and each other.

'Just like in the movies,' Peter remarked.

A short while later, two motorcycle cops bristling with guns, handcuffs and leather passed us.

'Just like in the movies,' said Jeff.

In Anaheim, we stayed at the Candy Cane Motel. (Where else?) With its giant red and white striped candy cane at the entrance, the pool, the multicoloured paintwork and decor – it was pure Californian kitsch. The promised Disneyland/Universal Studios visits lived up to everyone's expectations. I'm sure we didn't miss one ride. Even Jeff was warming to the travel caper by then!

In complete contrast, the next part of our adventure was a three-day drive from Vancouver to Calgary, where we hiked and explored the magnificent natural beauty of the Canadian Rockies.

Then it was on to Ottawa, and down to business. The Australian High Commission had booked us into the Four Seasons Hotel. Once again, the boys settled right into this luxury. They indulged in cable television, discovered all sorts of new takeaway food and made friends with the doorman, who wore a full-length mink coat on the chilly mornings and evenings.

Ray checked in for work. The geese had already flown south and the crisp autumn air sent us shopping for suitable winter clothes. We purchased a car, and I had to adapt quickly to driving on the wrong side of the road. I raced around looking for a house to rent for the year. It was a priority, as the Canadian school year was due to begin in just over a week and we needed an address before finding schools for the boys.

The house we found had a white marble entrance hall and a red-carpeted curved staircase leading upstairs.

When we first walked in, Stephen said, 'Yes, definitely like living in the movies!'

The two younger boys galloped off to explore the rooms and soon reappeared.

'It has a HUGE basement,' cried Peter.

'And a sauna,' said Rob.

'But no furniture,' said Jeff.

The High Commission gave me the address of a store which rented furniture and I set off that afternoon. I told the shop assistant my needs and the fact that I felt a bit overwhelmed by the task.

'Don't worry,' he said. 'We'll send our interior decorator out tomorrow to measure up the rooms and help you with your choices.'

And so, within a few days, we were settled in our lovely furnished home.

There was a primary school for Peter in the next block and a high school for the two older boys three blocks away. However, Rob would have to do the equivalent of year 8 at a separate intermediate high school, 1.4 kilometres away. No school bus from our house to his school presented a few problems on frozen, snowy mornings during the looming Ottawa winter.

A winter of constant sub-zero temperatures and heavy snowfalls. We listened at night to the snowplough clearing the streets and watched the ever-increasing snowbanks along the edges of the road. The boys learnt about shovelling snow to clear our driveway.

We had a slope in front of our garage, and one morning as I backed out, the snow tyres refused to take traction on the ice. The car slid down the drive, across the road and into the drive of the house opposite.

After that, Rob decided to walk to school, setting off in his balaclava, boots and snow gear, looking like Mawson in the Antarctic. Even more so when he returned each afternoon – stomping off the snow and ice at the back door, pulling off his scarf and balaclava to reveal icicled eyebrows and lashes, and demanding hot chocolate.

I was anxious for them all on their first day of school. We had heard that most of the kids purchased their lunches at the school cafeterias. (Just like in the movies!) I packed sandwiches and also gave them money to buy lunch if they thought it was a better alternative. Peter had already made friends with a boy who was in his class, so I felt he would be okay. The two older boys had each other to lean on. However, I worried about Rob.

Jeff and Stephen appeared at the house at lunchtime. 'A lot of the kids go home for lunch, Mum – so we did.'

That was fine, but I hopped in the car and drove to Rob's school. The school grounds were empty, except for one lone boy.

I tooted the horn. 'Do you want to come home for lunch?'

He came running across, 'Yes, please.'

We did this for the first two weeks, and then Rob settled in and made many friends. In fact, all the boys had an exceptional year at their respective schools, both academically and socially.

Not long after school started, our boxes arrived from home. I had a heavy cold, and it was a bleak, grey day when I opened a particular box. The smell of Australia filled the room. The eucalyptus bottle had broken.

I looked out at our leafless, birdless garden, momentarily transported home on the eucalyptus vapours in my nostrils. On the other side of the world, gum trees shimmering in the heat. Summer grass brown and crisp underfoot. Rosellas shrieking as they ripped bottle-brush to shreds, cicadas shrilling.

I was that little girl with a cold; my face lifted, mouth open to receive the communion of sugar, eucalyptus oil and attention I so craved from my father. I sniffed and blew my nose. Those blocked sinuses were clearing.

The boys came home from school one by one.

Peter, sniffing… 'I smell gum leaves!'

Robert, punching the air… 'Our stuff has arrived!'

Stephen, smiling broadly… 'Eucalyptus! The bush!'

Jeffrey, singing… 'This is Aust-rail-ee-a!'

I just smiled and gave them a Vegemite sandwich.

Camping With Crocs

'I believe we may have made a terrible mistake,' my husband whispered.

'Looks like a schoolies tour,' I said, biting my lower lip. I glanced around the small group gathered outside the Darwin Backpackers' Hostel. *What possessed me to book a couple of old retirees like us on an eight-day adventure camping safari, sleeping in swags with no tents and a bunch of young backpackers?*

Ray shrugged, 'Oh well, there's no going back now.'

We watched a battered twelve-seater four-wheel drive truck rumble around the corner, brakes squealing to a stop.

A bearded, muscular young man in brief khaki shorts, tattered bush hat and sturdy boots leapt out. 'Hi, I'm Leo, your driver, guide and cook. Who wants to go to Broome with a bit of adventure on the way?'

The energetic youth of the group punched the air and called, 'Yea!' while Ray and I stared apprehensively at our transport. *Would it make it to Broome?*

'C'mon, let's load the luggage and get this show on the road.' Leo climbed on top of the truck. 'Gunna be hot. Hope you all brought your swimmers.'

The Japanese girl looked alarmed. 'What about the dangerous crocodiles?'

'Don't worry, I won't let you swim near any crocs.'

From the start, this shy, Tokyo girl, Naoko, stuck very close to my side. I wondered about her travelling alone on such a trip and I know at times she found it quite a daunting experience. I can still see the horrified look on her face when Leo handed her the shovel and biodegradable toilet paper and explained the method of toileting in the outback.

We camped the first night near Lake Argyle. Leo unloaded the luggage and bedding and then showed us how to set up our swags. No tents, just swags on the ground, which proved extremely comfortable. With no barrier between us and the sky, each night we marvelled at the extraordinary, breathtaking spectacle of stars. Magic!

Leo produced a cask of white wine and whipped up a tasty meal for dinner. We sat on camp stools that balmy evening, two old crocks and young travellers from all around the globe, now becoming the best of mates.

Leo gave us a rundown on what to expect on the trip: staying mainly at rough bush camps, only one shower between here and Broome, but we could freshen up with swims along the way. 'In safe waterholes,' he said, looking at Naoko. We would start at dawn to make the most of each day.

'What time is dawn?' asked Naoko.

'A-ah, around five a.m.'

Next morning, we woke to the sound of an alarm clock at four thirty a.m. A chorus of expletives rang out, and a loud 'Who belongs to that?' from Leo.

'Solly, solly,' wailed Naoko.

A hail of shoes flew in her direction.

The air conditioning had broken down three hours out of Darwin, so we rumbled along with open windows through the red dust south of Kununurra until we reached the Bungle Bungle Ranges in Purnululu National Park, setting up camp late afternoon for our two-night stay. Ray and I enjoyed a cold beer and watched the kaleidoscope of colours reflected by the setting sun against the beehive-shaped domes in the distance. They reminded me of a family of wise old people. An ancient, all-knowing, mystical link with the land.

On our hike next day, a small whirlwind spiralled dust from the path ahead. My grandmother believed these willie-willies were spirits of the place. I imagined this one welcomed us as we trod with respect.

Fan palms clung to walls and crevices as we marvelled at the orange, yellow, black and grey stripes of the sandstone and conglomerate domes. What a place! What a day!

Early the next morning, we set off for a helicopter ride to view the whole mountain range from the air. When I saw the chopper had no side doors, I happily volunteered to take the middle spot. I gripped the pilot's seat in front of me with my knees and arms as we tilted, soared and dipped. My two companions, precariously secured only with seat belts, also clutched at the pilot's seat, and the three of us gasped in alarm each time we banked over and down for a better view.

'Spectacular!' cried Ray, but I could hear the terror in his voice.

That afternoon, we had one last walk in the Bungles. Our usually boisterous group moved silently, an inexplicable sense of calm and peace slowing our pace. Through a lush green gully, a narrow rocky chasm, on to the wonderful acoustics of Cathedral Gorge. There, after freshening up in the crystal-clear pool, we sat hushed as our young Welshman, Tom, sang 'Nessun Dorma' in his fine tenor voice. Life is full of extraordinary gifts.

We arrived late in the day at the next camp at Parry's Creek farm and set up beside a giant baobab tree near a picturesque billabong.

The local grazier pulled up in his ute. 'Don't any of you think of swimming down there,' he warned. 'I've set a trap for a big croc that took one of my dogs. Hope I'll catch him soon.'

Naoko's eyebrows shot up in terror. I shared her alarm.

'Leo,' I said, 'I'm not comfortable camping next to a billabong with a big croc.'

Leo assured us our camp was a safe distance from the water, but he could see I was not convinced. 'Judy, to prove I'm not worried, I'll put my swag between you and the billabong. Don't worry, I'll protect you.'

Next morning, I was the first to wake. Birds flitted and twittered around the still billabong water. I looked around. *No Leo.* I went searching and found him sound asleep in his swag way over behind the truck.

I gave him a kick, 'You said you'd protect us!'

He opened one eye and his mouth twisted into a wry grin. 'Judy,' he said, 'I lied.'

I wanted to kick him even harder.

'Did you sleep well?' he asked.

Later that day, we saw the brolgas dance.

A Mouthful of Ash

Marion would remember that period of their lives as the dark days. Shadowless, bleak, melancholy days when smoke filled her lungs and her mouth tasted of ash and destruction. Days when a thick grey haze blocked the sun and charcoal dust, blackened leaves and scorched dead birds fell upon the parched earth instead of the sweet rain they all craved.

It began the morning she spotted the billowing white cloud against the horizon. She called Bill, and they watched it turn grey and then black and spread across the sky.

They hurried inside and checked the fires-near-me app on their phones. All that day, they scanned the sky and website, alarm growing as the shadow grew both across the skies and on their screens. That was before the power failed and their phones went dead.

No power meant no pump for the water and sewerage on their remote bush block. They'd moved there, near the beach and national park, twenty-five years before. Paradise, they both decided. And paradise it was, until last year with Bill's cancer diagnosis followed by hideous months of surgery, chemo and radiation. They now teetered on a tightrope of hope, with neither daring to utter the word *remission*.

For the past year, they also watched disease spreading across their land. Devastation as fire spread across drought-stricken states, and politicians pontificated, fluffed about, then took off on vacation. Fires blazed in rainforests where they'd never burned before. Unbelievable loss of habitat, homes and life. Distressing scenes of people standing next to burnt-out houses, of koalas and kangaroos with pitiful charred feet and bodies. Disbelief as the disastrous infernos headed towards *them*, forming an arc to the north and west, then moving in to threaten their piece of paradise on the coast.

They fled just ahead of the approaching flames and for eight days camped on the oval near the town's evacuation centre, exchanging hugs and stories with their many friends also there. Unable to return to their homes because the fire still burnt out of control in an ever-growing perimeter around them.

Bill agonised over no longer being able to help his old volunteer rural fire group.

'No one expects you to be fighting fires, love,' Marion consoled. 'You did your bit for many years.'

On returning home they found that Bill's old RFS team had saved their house and the surrounding forest. Marion had always called this local bunch of firefighting volunteers 'Dad's Army'. With ages ranging between fifty and eighty, they all willingly gave up their time and energy to protect the community. *Unsung heroes.*

Marion and Bill drove to the fire station to thank their friends. They were told of the sudden wind change that turned things around as the fire jumped the lake and headed towards their area. The station bristled with activity as the radio crackled non-stop and the men and women of the brigade prepared to go out again, with their blackened uniforms and sooty, exhausted faces.

'What can we do to help?' asked Bill.

'Pray,' came the answer. 'We dodged a bullet here this time, but it's out of control to the north and west.'

Marion heard the judder, judder, judder of the helicopter long before she spotted it. She'd picked her way across the charcoal, ash and scorched leaves on the beach for a swim, longing for the cool sea, gasping for breath in the thick smoky air, wondering if it was worth the effort. The fire still burned a good fifteen kilometres away, but debris polluted the usually pristine seawater. She looked towards the fire-blackened headland to the north. One of their neighbours had walked up there at low tide yesterday and discovered a pile of burnt, dead wallabies and kangaroos on the rocks. The poor things had gone over the cliff trying to escape the fire.

Marion waded out, ducking under the foamy break. The helicopter whirred overhead, dipping its bucket towards the ocean. Something brushed against her shoulder and she gasped as she saw the dead bird. The pitiable creature bobbed on the wave as the chopper moved off. *Apocalypse now!*

Tom came from the city to stay for a while.

Bill placed a hand on Tom's shoulder, 'Good to see you, son.'

Marion observed them both. Her son, struggling with the depression that had plagued him for years. Her husband, struggling to understand their son's mental illness, frustrated at his own post-cancer frailty. Each battling his own demons.

The existing fire fronts spread and joined, cutting highways north, south and west. Tom couldn't leave now even if he wanted to. Petrol stations ran out of fuel. Supermarkets with no fresh produce. A power outage spread across the entire district. Shops and restaurants closed, food wasted or given away. Phones were useless. They relied on a battery-operated radio for news and lived on tinned and dried food.

'Didn't think I'd ever see Dad eating lentils by candlelight,' Tom grinned.

Marion prowled around at night, peered at the sky, longing to spy just one star in the smoke-blanketed heavens. The heat intensified; the winds shifty and the strain of watching and waiting rubbed on already raw nerves. Tensions grew in the house. They snapped at each other over trivial things, words spitting from mouths filled with ash. The residue of frictions smouldering for weeks.

The menacing flames returned and forced them to flee once again. The entire skyline glowed a fierce red as they neared the town.

'Madness,' cried Bill.

'The end of the world,' murmured Marion.

At the evacuation centre, people wandered around looking bewildered. Over three thousand jammed in together. Volunteers handed out comfort, food and drinks. More unsung heroes, Marion thought as she watched men and women busy in the kitchen, cars and trucks pulling up with food and supplies, two young tattooed girls heading in to clean the toilets with mops and buckets.

An elderly lady approached a weary young mother with a crying baby. 'Have you had any sleep, dear?'

'Not since we left our house at two this morning. My husband stayed to try to save the house. I haven't heard…' Her voice trailed off into a sob.

'I'll take the baby, dear. You put your head down for a bit.'

Caravans, campervans and tents filled the football ovals. People slept in their cars or on the evacuation centre floor. Young and old, rich and poor, dogs, cats, birds, even a miniature horse, all shrouded in uncertainty and the relentless thick grey smoke.

Helicopters and firefighting aircraft roared overhead. Fire trucks passed, lights flashing, the faces of the brave men and women inside grey with fatigue after months of fighting the endless flames. News of the navy evacuating people trapped on beaches further south filtered through. *War zone!*

Tom disappeared in the afternoon.

'Bet he's gone back with some crazy idea of saving the house or something.' Bill gave an exasperated sigh. 'Stupid bugger, I'll have to go and find him.'

'Over my dead body,' said Marion. She'd already hidden the car keys. They had a blazing row until she relented and handed them over. 'It's not safe, Bill,' she cried as he drove off. 'And hardly any petrol in the tank,' she muttered to the disappearing car.

Tom returned around nine p.m. 'Where've you been,' Marion asked? 'I've been worried sick.'

'I've been helping out. They had to evacuate everyone from the aged care home. No room here, so we took them over to the library. Those oldies are bloody stoic, Mum. Bedding down on the floor like kids at a school camp.'

Marion smiled. 'Some may have trouble getting up again.'

'Where's Dad?'

'He went looking for you. Thought you'd gone back to the house.'

'I couldn't get through. The road was closed.'

'Then where's your father?'

'They were only letting RFS and emergency people through. Oh shit, he doesn't still have his old RFS uniform, does he?'

After two anxious days with no word of Bill, a short section of the road north reopened. One lane still blocked, and only locals permitted through. They passed two burnt-out cars, twisted and melted beyond recognition.

'The heat must have been unimaginable,' Tom groaned.

Smoke still shrouded the air amidst the charcoal stencils of once-beautiful trees. Carbonised earth. Scorched dead animals. *Armageddon.*

Marion spotted the burnt-out car a few kilometres from their home. 'Oh no,' she groaned.

'Stay here, Mum,' Tom called as he scrambled out.

'Car's empty,' he gasped on his return. 'Let's hope he made it home.'

Marion slumped forward, her head in her hands. 'I can't take any more,' she said. 'The universe has gone mad. I'm sucked dry. Beaten to a pulp.'

Tom drove on slowly, dodging debris on the track until they reached the driveway, the flattened twisted fences, blackened remains of Marion's cherished garden, melted water tanks, burnt shed. But their home was intact.

On the veranda stood Bill. 'Lost the shed,' he said. 'But I managed to save the house.'

Making Do

A can of Rosella tomato soup, that's all Joan wanted. She wandered around for a considerable time before asking one of the Woolworth's staff where the soup aisle had gone.

'Aisle FIVE!' the girl shouted.

Joan winced. She knew most young people believed that all elderly folk were deaf, and now this 1.5-metre social distancing rule meant they yelled even louder.

Joan sighed and turned her trolley around. Last week soup was in aisle three next to dried fruits and flour. Today, the dried fruits had disappeared and the flour shelves were empty. *Was everyone at home in a frenzy of cake baking?* She had eventually discovered the dried fruits in aisle two, and placed her packet of prunes in the trolley, but the soup stock had vanished. The entire store, except for the meat and fresh produce, was rearranged! *Why did they do that?* Joan hated it. She was ninety-five years old, too old for change.

There was too much change in her life recently. First, the horrendous bushfires destroying homes, lives, flora and fauna, then the floods, and now this confounded coronavirus thing. Joan had survived a depression, wars, marriage, births and deaths, but this virus loomed strange and frightening. People out of work, lockdown, social distancing, the elderly isolated in nursing homes unable to see their families, folk sick and dying all over the world. Her mind was haunted by recent harrowing scenes on the television of body bags being loaded onto refrigerated trucks in New York City because the morgues were full. And all those pine coffins buried in trenches in mass graves on an island off Manhattan! What a sobering, tragic sight!

Joan remembered her visit to New York in 1987. She and Bob had been there for the Easter Parade. *Ah, New York!* The Statue of Liberty, Ellis Island, the Empire State Building., the Broadway shows. Bob kissing her passionately in the back of that yellow cab. The food, the smells, the noise, the hustle and bustle of the place. She found it difficult to imagine that such a vibrant, dynamic city, in a country like America, could be so helpless and under siege from the terrible virus. She wondered how long all this could go on.

Joan was glad she lived on the South Coast and not in the city.

Her son lived in Sydney and now worked from home because of the danger. 'Don't you go out, Mum. I'll organise for your groceries to be delivered.'

But Joan enjoyed her outing to Woolworths and decided she would continue to go while she could still drive. She'd hoped to see a few friendly faces during her shopping trip, but all her older friends seemed to be hunkering down at home and Joan noticed that people in the supermarket bore harassed, besieged expressions as they perused near-empty shelves.

Heavens above, her bridge sessions and U3A classes were cancelled and she couldn't visit the club for a meal or sit down in the coffee shop. The Indian chap at the coffee shop greeted her with a huge white-toothed smile when she called in for a takeaway coffee last week. Joan thought the empty chairs and tables at his coffee shop were probably the saddest sight she had encountered for a while. She resolved to buy a takeaway coffee every trip to town, even though it meant sitting in her car down by the river with only the seagulls for company. Yes, her routine had been thrown right out of whack, making her feel a bit discombobulated, and now this rearranging of the supermarket to make matters worse!

And the government was now spending money like it was going out of fashion. How would they pay it all back? Next, there would be a disastrous recession. Young ones today had no idea what might be in store for them. Young people today had no idea how to make do.

Joan could recall the last depression. The Great Depression, they had called it, spelt with a capital G and a capital D for good reason. A terrible time! She was only a small child but could remember her father leaving home to walk the track, searching for work to provide for his family. Joan knew they were lucky to live by the coast with a bit of land, and her mother kept a few hens and a vegetable garden to help keep them fed. There wasn't too much meat on their table in those days and the swaggies came to the back door begging for work or food. Joan watched her mother struggling to find something to give those poor men. Sometimes, it was simply a slab of bread with dripping and a few spoons of tea and sugar twisted into a piece of newspaper to send them on their way.

Joan recalled seeing a swaggie in the local general store one day. A half loaf of bread and one tomato sat on the counter in front of him. Mrs Baker weighed the tomato, wrapped the bread in tissue and told him the cost. The swaggie counted out his coins and was tuppence short. Mrs Baker repeated the amount needed and the poor man searched his pockets. He shook his head and Joan saw the awful despair in his eyes.

'Well, I'll have to make do with just the bread then,' he said, pushing the one tomato across the counter.

Mrs Baker took the coins and pushed the tomato back towards him. Dreadful, harsh times, those Depression days.

She pushed her trolley into aisle five, confronting the array of canned soups, dry packet soups, soups in lidded cups and now gourmet soups in pouches. '100% ORGANIC' they shouted. '100% AUS-TRALIAN.' Well, all that was well and good, but she still liked plain old tinned Rosella tomato soup. But where was it? Some Campbells and Heinz left on the shelves, but no Rosella. Joan felt like stamping her foot. *All this choice, but no Rosella!*

She picked up one of the fancy pouched soups and read: 'Organic tomatoes, grown without pesticides. GMO FREE' *(What did that mean?)*. 'NO SUGAR!' She put it back on the shelf and took a can of Heinz tomato soup. She would just have to make do with that, she supposed.

And now for the last thing on her list – some toilet paper.

Heading North

I rumble along the highway in the old Corolla, trying to ignore the waves of anxiety that knot my gut and force me to pull off the road just two hours into the journey. A truck passes, shaking me and the Corolla in its thundering wake. I get out and walk around a bit. Take lots of deep breaths and then set off again.

Mum insisted on buying me four new tyres before I left and I'm grateful for the thrum of the firm tread on bitumen as I steer around bends through the forest, mowing down tree shadows on the road. Through flickering spectres of light and shade as I crush the kilometres. Heading north. Far away from Dad's grim mouth and Mum's anxious eyes.

I watch the speedo. Don't want trouble. Aim to leave that behind. My sweaty hands clench the steering wheel as I try in vain to smother images of another journey long ago.

I eat at MacDonald's or Burger King when I can. No one expects you to make conversation in those places. Mind you, even couples and families don't talk to each other as they bend over their phone screens, thumbs flying, shovelling burgers and fries into voiceless mouths. My new phone sits in the glove box. I should take it out and charge it up, send a message home. But the habits of years of silence and detachment are hard to break. Years of learning how to retreat into isolation while moving through a crowd.

'The lights are on, but nobody's home,' one bloke muttered as the three of them pinned me against the wall of the showers.

They left me alone after that.

One day, I stop the Corolla outside a big supermarket. Mum took me to the local supermarket before I left, pointing out how things had changed. This one is unnervingly huge. So much light and noise! I shift from one foot to the other as I stand behind two young mums, their trollies loaded with groceries, toddlers whining for checkout treats. I decide to try the self-service express register with my two-minute noodles, chocolate milk and banana. Can't figure out how to scan the banana, so I leave it. Need to get out of there fast. The beeps of the registers freak me out. Remind me of the beep-beep-beeping in the hospital that night.

The night we headed north out of Batlow in Dad's new Holden ute. I peered forward through the high beam at the dark winding road. Johnno in the front beside me, girls lying over in the back. We were all drunk.

'Dad told me never to ride in the back of a ute,' Kylie giggled as she and Emma clamoured in over the tailgate and collapsed in a heap on the mattress.

We had thrown the old foam mattress in at the last minute.

Just in case. 'Never know your luck,' Johnno said at the time.

We sped along the narrow road, eyes peeled for roos or wombats.

Johnno slapped the dash twice with one palm and laughed his hyena laugh. 'Those girls are legless, man. We're right tonight!'

But nothing went right that night.

It's easy to find work as a kitchen hand or labourer as I head further north. I am polite, clean-cut and muscled up. Years of practice to perfect that.

A dark-haired Belgium girl in the youth hostel in Yamba leads me to her room, locks the door and kisses me. She pulls away and flings herself backwards onto the mattress, laughing. For a moment, I stare at her lying there, her body twisted towards me.

'Come,' she says, beckoning and giggling.

I turn, fumble with the lock, and scramble through the doorway. Run along the beach and howl in the darkness.

I dial up the volume on the radio the next morning as I head out of Yamba. Winding down the window, I breathe in the fresh air and listen to music I like.

For five years I shared with a big, tattooed bloke who only played AC/DC. I once loved Acca Dacca, but five years of 'Highway to Hell' is more than anyone can take.

In Murwillumbah, a café owner tells me of work on an organic farm outside town. 'Two *ladies* run the place.' He taps the side of his nose with one finger as he says *ladies* and gives me a nod. 'They grow avocados and various fruits and vegetables. Probably could use a bit of extra muscle for a while with the harvesting.'

Joan and Maggie are middle-aged and businesslike. They quiz me about my experience and I watch them size me up with their calm, direct looks. Then Joan turns to Maggie with a smile and a nod and they show me to a granny flat in the backyard.

'You have a jug, toaster, microwave and fridge,' Maggie tells me. 'You take care of your breakfast and lunch and we'll provide a meal at night. We eat a lot of vegetarian food. All organic, good stuff. But we do have some fish and chicken. Feel free to join us for dinner or have your meals in your flat. It's up to you, Matt.'

Turns out Joan used to be a naturopath and she takes my hand and examines my fingernails. 'You've been on the road too long, eating too much junk food. We'll soon sort that out.'

Maggie is a really good cook and I've never tasted vegetarian like she dishes up. The place is isolated and peaceful, and they leave me to myself. I sit on the plastic chair outside my little place at night, delaying going to bed and the unwelcome dreams. I smoke in the dark, listen to the night sounds and look at the sky. I haven't seen stars for years, and the only night sounds I've heard were snores and groans and the screams of my nightmares.

After I've worked there for three weeks, Joan asks me to go with her into town to help with deliveries. On the way home, we round a bend to see a ute on its roof, wheels spinning in the air. Joan hits the brakes, leaps out onto the road. Runs towards the vehicle. I'm frozen. My bum superglued to the seat.

Joan comes rushing back, takes one look at my face and realises I'm not going to be much help. She bites her lip, leans in towards me and grabs the first-aid kit from the glovebox. 'Matt, we need medical assistance. There's no phone reception out here. I'll do what I can. You have to drive to town to the police station. Tell them we're out on the Tyalgum Road near Stoney Creek Road.'

The next morning, I tell Joan and Maggie that I'll be moving on at the end of the week.

'We'll miss you,' Joan says. She takes my hand and examines my nails. 'Better,' she nods. 'Your body is healing.' She hesitates, looks me in the eye, 'Matt, whatever's troubling your mind will heal also, you know, with time.'

Maggie hugs me on the day I leave and presses a slip of paper into my hand. 'Here's the address of friends up near Woodford. They run an organic farm and would welcome your help.'

Johnno now lives in Townsville with his wife and two children. Can't imagine him as a family man. He wrote and invited me to come, said there was a job if I needed one. I slowly work my way up the coast, all the while debating if I should take up his offer. I convince myself he can't really want to see me. And do I want to see him? Stir up all that old shit? But I keep travelling north.

A Spanish couple I meet in the youth hostel in Bundaberg discover I have a car and ask if I will give them a lift to the Mon Repos Turtle Centre on the coast. We join a group of tourists and that night watch the loggerhead turtle hatchlings struggle across the sand towards the sea. The ranger tells us that only one in a thousand will reach maturity.

An old bloke standing beside me shakes his head, 'Look at them go! Each one of those little buggers is so determined to grab on to life.

Makes you think, doesn't it? Makes you think how precious life is…
and how fragile.'

*Emma screamed by the side of the road – a piece of jagged bone protruding
from her leg – glistening white in Johnno's shaking torchlight. It was a while
before we found Kylie lying limp and twisted on her back on the paddock
grass.*
   'She's still breathing, man.'
   But her body lay in a strange position.
   'Shit, shit, shit!' Johnno cried.

Early next morning, I drive alone back out to Mon Repos and walk
along the deserted beach. I see the myriad of tracks across the sand
where a highway of tiny beings made their way to the sea the previous
night and wonder why only some are destined to survive. *Where's the
justice in it all?* I ask myself. *Where's the justice?*
   The sobs rise in my throat as I wade out. I clench my fists, arms rigid
by my side as the warm ocean laps around my waist, my chest, my neck.

*Manslaughter was the worse sentence I could have got, but I deserved it. I
killed Kylie, no doubt about that. I condemned her parents to a lifetime of
grief. Her father sent me an abusive letter telling me he would never forgive
me for murdering his daughter and wished I would rot in hell. But I was
already there.*

The water is clear, warm, inviting. It's so easy to keep walking. I'm calm
and determined as I taste the salt against my lips. I hear people yelling,
but I keep going, my eyes fixed on the horizon.
   The shouting gets louder. 'Hey, Matt, Matt!' It's the Spaniards. They
are calling, laughing, splashing around me.

A week later, I drive three times past the house before I dare to stop the
car. I get out and walk up the front path.

We stand a distance apart, Johnno and I, when he opens his door. I struggle to control the tremor in my voice as I say 'Hello.'

Children somewhere in the house emit squeals of laughter. A female voice calls out in the background. As I unclench my fists, I tell myself it was a mistake to come here. *Another terrible, stupid mistake.*

Johnno steps forward. He clasps my half-outstretched hand and draws me to him. Wraps his other arm around my back. Laughs his hyena laugh. 'Welcome, bro. Welcome.'

The Quintessential Mrs Barton-Hall

Dorothy took immense pride in her orderly house. Her expert eye ensured everything was in impeccable symmetry. Table settings sat perfectly aligned, as were the neat shrubs in her garden. She arranged furniture in painstaking balance, and guests usually perched stiffly on the edge of her upright chairs.

No one could fold fitted sheets to such flat, razor-sharp edges as Dorothy Barton-Hall. After giving each sheet a satisfied pat, she placed it to sit obediently in the orderly rows of linen in her hall closet.

Friends were accustomed to Dorothy rising from her chair in the middle of a conversation to straighten a flower in a vase or a painting on a wall. One friend, Prue, occasionally set Dorothy's place at luncheons or dinners with a spoon missing or a steak knife instead of a fish knife. She knew how much pleasure it gave Dorothy to correct such mistakes.

Dorothy was proud to be the wife of a prominent barrister. She kept a close watch on Malcolm's cases, and his work often offered something to drop into conversations during tête-à-têtes with friends. Malcolm was steady, reliable, predictable. Until last year, when he arrived home with tickets for a cruise on the *Queen Mary* from Singapore to Hong Kong as a surprise to celebrate their fortieth wedding anniversary. Dorothy didn't like surprises, and she discovered she didn't like cruise ships either, no matter how luxurious or how much her friends expressed their envy. In fact, she was completely and literately at sea on a ship where every little thing was meticulously organised and controlled by others. Dorothy didn't like that at all, but that didn't stop her from bragging to her friends about how wonderful everything had been on her return.

Two charities considered themselves fortunate to have Dorothy Barton-Hall on their board of directors. A tireless worker, she bullied acquaintances into raising money for her charities with a rallying 'Come on, keep working, we can do it!' Her recent nomination for an award for outstanding charity work surprised no one, the ceremony scheduled at Government House the following month.

Dorothy shopped many hours for the right outfit to wear to the award ceremony and finally settled on a smart navy suit with matching navy shoes. However, the choice of blouse had been the source of dilemma. White was too ordinary, too business-like and old fashioned. Red, much too brash. Pale aqua was a possibility. She had the Perri Cutten shop at Double Bay hold a nice aqua shirt for three days. Then she discovered a lovely cerise number. The saleswoman proclaimed that it did 'wonders for the complexion' and Dorothy agreed that it was perfect: bright, fashionable and tasteful.

One morning as Dorothy straightened Malcolm's tie before he left the house, she noticed he looked tired and distracted. She made a mental note to ask him about it that night over their pre-dinner g and t.

She settled down with the *Sydney Morning Herald*. It was important to keep up with current affairs. A headline on the second page caught her eye. 'Mother charged with murder of disabled son,' with Malcolm's name as defence barrister. Dorothy read further…

She was particularly fastidious with Malcolm's meal that night. However, she didn't mention the murder trial.

The week before the ceremony at Government House, Malcolm announced he would be unable to attend. 'I'm very sorry, my dear, but I have an important day in court which I cannot postpone.' He looked across at his wife's crestfallen face. 'You must have read about it! The murder of the disabled boy.'

'Well, if it's important to you,' Dorothy sniffed.

Malcolm hesitated, biting his lower lip. 'You realise our Richard would have been thirty-five this month?'

Dorothy nodded. She stiffened, folded her arms across her chest, trying to disguise the trembling that quaked through her body.

Malcolm closed his eyes for a moment and sighed. 'I'm sorry, but the case is very important. This woman cared for her severely disabled son for thirty years. She fed him, saw to his needs twenty-four hours every day. She devoted her entire life to him. She's now suffering from terminal cancer and ended her son's life because she feared no one would care for him after her death. It's a tragic affair and I cannot let her down.'

Dorothy cleared the table, loaded the dishwasher, then drew herself a deep bath. She excelled in clearing her mind of clutter, but the image of a small baby with twisted limbs kept reappearing; no matter how deeply she breathed in the perfume of the lavender candles and lavender-oil infused bathwater.

Thirty-five years ago. The terrible birth. The grave prognosis. Her inability to cope.

Malcolm had visited Richard in the home every week. The boy's eyes sparkled at the sight of his father. Dorothy hovered in the background. The child became distressed whenever she touched him. He made the most awful sounds, drooling, spitting and thrashing around. Several times, this developed into an awful seizure. It proved too painful for all of them, and so Dorothy stopped going. When Richard passed away at six years old, she organised a beautiful funeral. Everyone said how tasteful it was.

Dorothy organised Prue to drive them both to Government House for the award ceremony. She heard the car pull into the driveway and looked at her watch with an exasperated sigh. Prue had arrived twenty minutes early. Dorothy hadn't slept well the previous night and now, here was Prue sitting in the driveway twenty minutes before schedule!

They had a good run through the traffic and arrived much too early.

Dorothy made Prue drive around the block several times. 'Being early is as bad as being late,' she said.

The lunch was perfect and Dorothy made a mental note of the menu and flower arrangements as she straightened the knife and fork of her place setting. She adjusted the sleeves of her jacket. Yes, she was very pleased with her outfit and noticed several of her friends and quite a few strangers look her up and down as they nodded and remarked to each other. The cerise blouse was an excellent choice.

The ceremony began. Dorothy's chest swelled with pride when the Governor announced, 'For outstanding fundraising work for the Cerebral Palsy Alliance and Association for Children with Disability – Dorothy Barton-Hall.'

All eyes were upon Dorothy weaving her way through the tables to the platform. Three steps to negotiate. She kept her back straight and firm, but glanced down briefly to make sure she didn't stumble on the first step. It was then she discovered she was wearing one navy and one black shoe.

To the Sea

'To the sea, to the sea,' called Tom, racing ahead down the pathway with his mother in the wheelchair.

'To the sea,' Helen echoed, laughing, as she mimicked the old catch cry of their father so long ago...

'To the sea,' Owen had always called as the family crammed into the car.

Driving from Canberra down the mountain, they all waited and strained for that first glimpse of the ocean through the trees.

'There it is!'

They would then argue over who saw it first until finally, Joy cried, 'Stop, or there'll be no fish and chips.'

Oh! I do like to be beside the seaside
I do like to be beside the sea...

Joy was born by the sea. Her mother had died when Joy was two years old. Her father was a carpenter. 'Like Jesus,' Joy told people when she was young.

He loved the outdoors and the sea in particular. 'Come on, girlie,' he'd cry as he hoisted Joy onto his shoulders, 'let's go to the beach.'

As a small child, she paddled in the shallows and watched with awe as her father's big muscular body swept towards her on a wave. He taught her to swim and later to body surf. Joy could still recall the first time he lifted her onto a wave and shouted, 'Go!' She kicked furiously and then realised that there was no need to swim as she was propelled gloriously forward. There was a soft roar as water filled her ears and bubbles swept up her nose. The force of the wave tumbled her over and unceremoniously plonked her on the sandy shore. *Oh, the thrill of being suspended on that wave!* From that moment on, she couldn't get enough.

Growing up, she spent every spare minute swimming and surfing.

'You'll grow gills,' her father warned.

Once, a savage rip caught her unawares. She knew what to do: *Don't struggle, stay calm.* Then she saw the fin! *Punch its nose. Poke its eyes.* She tried to remember all the advice she'd heard about shark attacks. She saw three more dark shapes and realised they were dolphins. They swam with her. All fears vanished as they played around her, guiding her to safety. Joy's friends all rolled their eyes when she told the story, but her father believed it.

By the sea, by the sea, by the beautiful sea,
You and I, you and I. Oh, how happy we'll be…

When she was eighteen, she met a sandy-haired, blue-eyed boy.

'Hook, line and sinker,' her father muttered as she rushed out the door to meet Owen one night.

It was a salty romance, and they dived headlong into those dreamy froth and bubble days! They stole shy, briny kisses on the sand, plunged through the breakers, enjoying the surf and baking themselves for hours in the sun. Something Joy bitterly regretted many years later when she noticed the mole on Owen's back.

After their marriage, Owen acquired a job in Canberra. Joy busied herself making their new home comfortable, but sometimes she discovered herself standing still, facing the direction of the coast. She sniffed the dry Canberra air that parched her skin and body summer and winter, longing for moisture, salt, and the sustenance of the sea.

She found work in a haberdashery store and became proficient at helping fastidious sewers choose fabrics, the right shade of thread, and the perfect button or trim. She made herself a deep blue silk organza gown, embroidered with crystal beads. It shimmered and sparkled as

Owen swept her around the ballroom floor. He smiled and whispered that dancing with her in that iridescent blue dress almost made up for being away from the ocean.

They made the trip down the mountain to the seaside as often as they could, boisterously singing all the way, and the old Austin always boiled on the journey back. They slept tangled together in their little tent, Owen's sunburnt arm slung across Joy's waist. Eventually, they bought a caravan and left it on-site at the coast after the twins, Helen and Tom, arrived.

Those were such happy days! Carrying salty wet bundles back from the beach, they dumped the babies into the laundry tub at the caravan park to wash sand, salt, and grime from chubby crevices. Joy loved the delicious smell of those clean little bodies after their swim and a bath. Then small hands grabbed their buckets and spades and headed back for more.

Later, as the children grew older, Owen announced there was enough for a deposit on a small beach cottage.

Red sails in the sunset, way out on the sea,
I'm far from my loved one, who's waiting for me...

Joy moved to the beach cottage after Owen died. Helen had married a coastal man and lived nearby. Tom came with his family from Canberra for the holidays. Joy loved her grandchildren and observed their progress from buckets, spades, and floaties to wetsuits and surfboards.

One Christmas lunch, as the whole family gathered at Helen's; Joy sat quietly listening to the rowdy banter and suddenly felt superfluous. Invisible. She went to the bathroom and looked at her thin, wrinkled face in the mirror and thought, *I'm disappearing. Shrivelling up like an old lump of sun-dried seaweed.* She scolded herself for being so maudlin and decided to have a swim.

Helen's daughter, Sandy, saw Joy go past the side window. 'Gran's off for a swim.'

Helen laughed, 'Well, that's one way to get out of the washing up!'

Sandy ran to the open window, 'Hey, Gran, wait for me!'

A few years later, Helen placed her own new granddaughter in Joy's arms. 'Look, Mum, your first great-grandchild has Dad's feet.'

Joy balanced the tiny foot in her hand. The second toes were longer than the first, just like Owen's. Joy gently stroked the child's smooth cheek with the knuckle of one bent, arthritic finger.

'Her name is Emma Joy,' said Sandy.

For I'm dancing with tears in my eyes
'Cause the girl in my arms isn't you…

She tried to call out to them as they gathered around the hospital bed. Joy could see her family standing there, concern and horror in their eyes. She heard every word they said.

She struggled to move her hands and feet, struggled to open her mouth. 'I'm all right,' she screamed, but no one understood.

Trapped in her useless body, she was unable to communicate. Unable to do anything. She lay there, day after day, in the hard, narrow, nursing home bed, completely reliant on others. Her pad soaked with urine (or worse) until a nurse found time to change it. Each morning, they attached her to the lifter and hoisted her like a lump of meat from the bed. They lowered her limp old body onto a cold plastic chair in the bathroom, stripped her down, soaped her up and then hosed her with the showerhead. *Oh, the indignity of it all!* Joy hated it and lay there remembering the days when she could sing, dance, laugh and run across the sand towards the sea. When she was buoyant and free…

'Nanna, Great-gran's crying,' Emma called.

Helen wiped the tears from her mother's cheeks and dribble from the slack old mouth. 'What is it, Mum? Please don't cry,' she begged as she fought back her own tears.

Emma climbed onto the bed. 'She wants a cuddle,' she said and promptly went to sleep, her chubby arm slung across her great-grandmother's waist.

Helen stood looking at her mother and granddaughter on the bed. Her greatest joy was caring for Emma during the week while Sandy worked, and they visited Joy each afternoon. Helen hated these visits. She hated every time she walked into the room and saw her mother's eyes.

However, Emma made it easier. Everyone in the nursing home loved the child, and she did not seem to mind the ancient claw-like hands clutching out at her as she passed.

'Dance for us, Emma,' the old people cried as they gathered in the recreation room for the sing-along.

The child swayed and twirled to the sounds of sweet aged voices singing, *I'm forever blowing bubbles,* and all the bygone songs they knew so well; even if they couldn't remember what they'd eaten for lunch minutes earlier.

Helen often pushed the wheelchair along the path of the nursing home garden to the rotunda by the cliff.

Emma stood holding Joy's hand as they looked towards the sea. 'She likes it here.'

It was a welcome escape from the smell of urine, decrepitude and death, and they often saw the dolphins.

Wish me luck as you wave me goodbye
Cheerio, here I go, on my way…

Tom had sped down the mountain from Canberra to the nursing home. He bent, kissing the tissue-thin skin of his mother's cheek. He took some ice, rubbing it across her dry, cracked lips. 'What is it, Mum?' He bent closer, trying to make sense of the jumbled sounds.

'She wants to see the sea,' said Emma matter-of-factly.

'Darling, she's too sick today.' Helen lifted the child onto her lap.

'Why not?' demanded Tom.

'Tom, she's dying.'

'Precisely!'

'They won't let us.'

'We won't ask!'

Tom lifted his mother from the bed, horrified at the weightlessness of her body. He remembered the strength of her arms as she supported him in the water, teaching him to swim. How she sometimes held his face between her hands and looked with love into his eyes. He swallowed hard, trying to hide the sob rising in his throat. Helen coughed and fussed, tucking Joy into the wheelchair.

'To the sea,' said Tom as he released the brake on the chair.

Then they rushed out the side door and down the path. They huddled close together at the top of the cliff.

Emma looked up at the reflection of blue sky and sea rippling across Joy's glasses. She felt a tremor from the old withered hand as she asked, 'Can you see the dolphins, Great-gran?'

Hard Love

Empty plate, empty pockets, empty mind. Two days until the next dole payment. He knew he could get a meal that night from the Salvos. He knew all the free food and handout places around the city. He was lucky; he had a place in the squat. A place to sleep. Lots didn't.

His mother came often. At first, she begged him to come home, but not lately. She brought food and sometimes clothes. She never gave him money any more. He'd emptied all her trust the last time he OD'd.

Luke sat slumped with his face in his hands. *What a fucked-up, empty life!*

Carol locked her office door and set off through the bustling crowds. The path from her workplace to the squat on the edge of the city took her past the local dealers and users. She looked out for Luke and was relieved when he wasn't there. Most weeknights, she wandered for a while through the city streets and alleys searching for him, her heart lurching when she saw a figure slumped in a laneway. But some nights lately, she just didn't have the energy. The users all knew her. They sometimes told her where he was – sometimes not. Their loyalties divided between Luke and what they knew was her love for him. A mother's unconditional love for her child.

Luke had a child of his own, and Carol knew he loved his daughter. He'd loved Anna once also, but she'd issued an AVO against him when Jade was three years old. Things had gone sour – drugs and money problems, mainly. It happened after the night he came home to find the house locked. He saw Jade, her fingers splayed against the window, crying, 'Daddy, Daddy.' He picked up a brick and smashed the glass panel on the front door.

Sam had noticed it first, years ago. He tried to help his brother before coming to her. 'Luke needs help, Mum. He's really into drugs.'

She'd tried every avenue since then, but nothing worked.

Sam finished his science degree and fled to a job in Queensland. Carol didn't blame him. She felt like running away herself.

'You must give Luke hard love, Carol,' the counsellor told her. 'Step back and never blame yourself.'

Huh! What did he know? Had he ever had to change the locks because his son stole every item he could lift to get money for drugs? Had he ever cradled his unconscious son and waited for the ambulance? How many sleepless nights had he spent wondering? Please, someone, wake me up when this nightmare is all over.

The loud ding-dong of the doorbell startled Carol as she was getting ready to leave for work. She found Anna and Jade at her front door.

'Luke will be here soon, Carol. Can you look after Jade until he comes?' Anna kissed her daughter and was gone.

Carol watched her get into an old ute, giving the driver an exuberant hug before they drove off with a skid and a roar. She took Jade's backpack, surprised at its weight. 'Hey, beautiful, what've you got in here?'

'All my clothes.'

Carol took a deep breath, took Jade to the kitchen, sat her down to cereal and milk, and phoned the office to say she'd be late. She dialled Luke's number but got the 'this number is out of service' message.

Two hours later, Luke burst through the front door, bristling with agitation and panic. 'Mum, Anna's pissed off. Sent me a note saying I must look after Jade. Said she'd left her here with you.'

Carol paused – *hard love, how hard could hard love be?*

'Jade, let's find a DVD for you to watch.'

She observed the hunched shoulders of her son as he paced around.

She knew the signs, knew his total focus at that moment was on getting his next hit. Something to take him away from the present crisis. She made coffee for them both and took it out to the patio.

Luke's hands shook as he tried to roll a cigarette. 'Mum, can we stay here until I work something out? I can't take her to the squat.'

'I'll give you two weeks, Luke. No drugs. You must straighten yourself out. You have to. Jade is your responsibility. I'm not going to look after her. You have to do that. She's your daughter.' She took a deep breath. She was resolved. *Hard love!* 'Think about it, Luke. Think about it! Do you want to see her grow up? What memories of her father do you want her to have? She'll end up in child protection if you don't straighten yourself out.'

A few days later, she found the needles and heroin hidden in his room. She'd gone looking while he and Jade were at the park. He'd been just too together, too soon. She knew him too well. Sam happened to phone at that moment, and she couldn't control her misery and tears.

When Sam offered to pay for the plane tickets to Queensland, Luke realised his brother was throwing him the last lifeline. Sam lived miles out of town. No temptations and no judgements here, Sam had guaranteed.

Luke was astounded when his mother refused to take care of Jade while he went to Queensland.

Carol stood; fists clenched. 'No. She's your responsibility. Not mine, not Sam's. Yours.' She felt a surge of terror, imagining all the horrors that might await Jade, but she knew that this was Luke's last chance. She fought back the tears, her body tense and trembling; sensing that if her son stepped forward and touched her at that moment, she would disintegrate into a million brittle shards on the floor.

Jade peered out the plane window as the plane soared above the city. Luke couldn't get the seal off the orange juice because his hands were shaking so badly. The woman next to him pretended not to watch.

Jade turned from the window and took the cup. 'I'll help you, Daddy.' She prised open the foil seal with her small white teeth and set the container down on the tray. Then she carefully peeled back the lid. 'There you are, Dad.'

'You're so lucky to have such a good little helper,' said the woman in the aisle seat.

'Yes, I am.' Luke drained his juice and placed the empty cup back on the tray.

The Golden Thread

I wandered through the corridors of the hospital, lost and confused. People zipped past, conversing in rapid Italian, all intent on pursuing important tasks. Busy. Passing and talking. Lips moving rapidly in a language I didn't understand. *Very excitable, animated people, these Italians.*

The signs on the walls meant nothing to me in this foreign place. *Which way to go?* I felt bewildered and alone. I longed for a golden thread to guide me through this labyrinth of a hospital.

My fingers ran along the delicate chain around my neck, down to the gold replica of an ancient Minoan disc. Bruce gave it to me one radiant morning in Crete over fifty years ago. I'd worn it constantly since, habitually caressing it whenever lost in thought or needing comfort.

We met at a youth hostel in Verona. Two young Aussie strangers who had journeyed across the globe to meet and fall in love. We travelled together through Italy and Greece until that day in Crete when he asked me to marry him.

'This is until I can afford a ring,' Bruce promised as he fastened the chain around my neck.

The owner of the jewellery shop beamed a gold-toothed smile. He hadn't expected a sale from two young scruffy-looking backpackers. 'Ah, my little Ariadne and Theseus,' he murmured. 'I wish you much happiness.'

I knew the story of Ariadne's love for Theseus. The ball of thread she gave him to find his way out of the labyrinth after he had slain the Minotaur. 'Didn't Theseus later abandon Ariadne on Naxos?'

'Ah, but he came back for her.'

But we both knew Ariadne had died by then.

'What do the signs on the medallion mean?' asked Bruce.

The store owner seemed relieved to change the subject. 'It is a replica of a disc of fired clay found in the ruins of the palace of Phaistos. The signs have proven to be indecipherable.' The shopkeeper smiled and nodded. 'Like a woman.'

I turned yet another corner in the hospital. *Would I never see my husband again in this hideous maze of a place?* I had not wanted to leave Bruce the previous night, disturbed by the diagnosis from the *one* doctor who spoke English. *Six fractured ribs. A punctured lung. Possible liver damage. Maybe need for surgery…* But the doctor declared there was nothing I could do by staying.

It was the first day of the European holiday to celebrate our fiftieth wedding anniversary and retrace some of the steps of our youth. After the two-hour drive from Venice airport, we were getting ready for dinner when I heard the thud and a loud bellow from the bathroom. Bruce slipped while stepping into the bathtub to take a shower. He crashed down, smashing his side on the edge of the tub.

'I'm all right,' he wheezed, 'perhaps a broken rib…or two.'

However, he appeared anything but all right. I demanded we seek some kind of medical help. The hotel manager gave us directions to the nearest hospital, two kilometres north on the freeway and Bruce insisted he could drive.

I wasn't insured to drive the hire car. Before we left home, I had been adamant that I would not drive in Europe and only Bruce's name was on the rental agreement. So now I watched helplessly, as my husband, pale and sweating and in obvious pain, lowered himself gingerly into the little manual Ford Fiesta.

As he lay in the emergency room bed, full of morphine, Bruce insisted I must drive the car back to the hotel, slurring out a few instructions on shifting gears and emphasising the importance of the clutch. 'They'll tow away the car if we leave it in the hospital car park,' he said.

It was over fifty years since I had driven a manual car. The Fiesta stalled and bucked around the car park on a short practice run before I felt brave enough to venture out onto the road, still in second gear. Fortunately, there was little traffic about at midnight. I took a wrong turn and ended up heading west instead of east on the freeway. It was ages before the next exit enabled me to go back. I leant forward, peering ahead, teeth gritted, praying that no police appeared to stop me and discover that I shouldn't be driving that wretched little car. My neck and jaw ached, the steering wheel slippery with the sweat of my clenched palms.

Back in the hotel room, the air conditioning didn't seem to work, and the night was unbearably hot. I couldn't sleep as my mind galloped through all the worst possible scenarios. At two a.m., I got up and studied the instructions for making an international call on the hotel room phone before dialling the reverse charge number listed on the travel insurance policy.

'Alliance Insurance, Craig speaking.' Craig's broad rough Aussie accent embraced me like a blast of Sydney sunshine. My new best friend Craig informed me he would take care of everything. 'Australia and Italy have a reciprocal health care agreement,' he said. 'So, your medical costs should be minimal. I can help you with hotel cancellations, flights home – whatever's necessary.' He advised me to get some sleep and phone again after I revisited the hospital.

The next morning, I discovered a rash around my neck and chest. Anxious and a little breathless, I now also had a pain in my upper back. 'Get a grip, woman,' I told myself.

'Can you not drive?' the hotel manager enquired when I asked him for directions to walk to the hospital.

I gave him an adamant 'no'.

'It is more complicated to *walk* to the hospital than to drive.'

'I cannot drive.'

'The weather is hot today. I can call you a taxi,' he suggested.

He was young. I realised that his forty-year-old eyes were looking at an old woman in her seventies. However, this old woman was stubborn. I walked a four-kilometre route at home most mornings.

'I can walk there,' I insisted.

The manager shrugged and sketched out a map, patiently explaining the many twists and turns through the streets to the hospital.

Back at the emergency department, after several failed attempts at communication, the triage nurse found a young doctor who spoke English. He made a series of telephone calls and then directed me to the surgical ward in block C.

The place was a maze of passageways and buildings. Why did block A lead to block D? *What happened to B and C?* Eventually, I discovered block C and stood in front of the huge directory signboard, trying to guess the Italian for *surgical*. I had no idea.

I squared my shoulders and set off. Bruce was somewhere on one of the four floors of block C. I tried to ignore the mounting sense of helplessness as I constantly fingered the chain on my neck.

Around a corner came an orderly pushing Bruce in a wheelchair. My knees buckled with relief. My big strong Bruce, looking so vulnerable with his hairy legs sticking out of the too-short hospital gown.

'I've just had yet another X-ray,' he said. 'I've had no sleep. I've been in and out of X-rays all night.' He looked pale and ill and grimaced in pain as the orderly bumped the wheelchair into a lift.

We reached Bruce's hospital room to find two women and a man waiting. They bombarded us with a barrage of indecipherable Italian. We shrugged and raised our palms in bewilderment.

Then a wonderful English-speaking nurse called Rosa showed up and explained that the doctors were awaiting various results to determine if surgery was necessary. In the meantime, the administration officer needed Bruce's passport and Australian Medicare card. But, of course, they were in the safe back at the hotel.

'You have a nasty rash,' Rosa remarked, peering at my neck. 'You should remove that chain.'

'I never take it off.'

Rosa frowned and shook her head. I hesitated, but then unclipped the clasp and slipped the chain and disc into my purse.

The racket of cicadas was deafening as I trudged back towards the hotel to collect the required paperwork. It was early afternoon, not a taxi anywhere, the entire area deserted for the lunchtime siesta. I followed my map in reverse. On the way to the hospital that morning, I made a mental note of several shops as a reference guide. Now with shop shutters closed, the streets sucked dry of cars and people, everything looked so different. The heat was horrendous.

An old man appeared.

'*Scusi*,' I said, pointing to my map.

He peppered me with a torrent of Italian and waved his hands about, indicating I should go further to the right. Unsure, I followed his directions.

The cicadas ratcheted on as I plodded along in the searing afternoon sun. My head was muddled from lack of sleep, jet lag and the trauma of Bruce's accident. *I was lost.* Tightening my aching shoulders, I turned to retrace my steps back to the hospital to start again.

The suicidal song of a million cicadas jackhammered into my brain. They sang to attract a mate. The louder they sang, the more chance they had to lure a partner *or* a predator.

My feet were sore and swollen, my neck itched, my back throbbed, and the tightness in my chest made it hard to breathe.

The cicadas now seem to have stopped their screeching. The pain in my back and chest skewers me to the scorching pavement. I lie here like a helpless insect. A group of chattering people hover over me. Very excitable, animated people, these Italians…

My fingers reach for the chain around my neck; the tactile comfort of the familiar signs on my precious Minoan disc. It is not there.

The Old Brownie Box

I find it in a box of old belongings in the garage. It is black and solid in my hands. There is a loud *click-clack* when I press the side button. I remember the wonder and delight when I opened the Christmas present from Aunty Una. It was 1954, and I was eleven...

I had never received such an expensive gift: A Brownie Box Six-20 camera, made in England by Kodak Limited. None of my family owned a camera. The few photos we possessed were taken by the street photographers around Sydney in those days. They snapped photos as we left Town Hall station or walked along the Manly Corso, handing Mum the ticket, as they knew she would be the most likely to buy. 'Ready tomorrow, missus – at this address.'

I pull out the winder on the side of the old camera and open the back, remembering how the roll of black and white 620 films had to be carefully slotted in and wound on slowly, preferably in a darkened room because of the risk of exposure. I learnt to be frugal and careful with my photo-taking, because of the expense of both the film and processing. There was little cash to spare in our working-class household and it was Mum who scraped together the money for film and developing. She said those family photos were important.

Aunty Una came into our lives when I was six years old. I remember her bustling into the room wearing a starched white uniform and veil, my new baby sister in her arms. She owned and ran a private maternity hospital in the Sydney suburb of Five Dock, and my four younger sisters and brothers were all born there.

A brisk, upright, well-corseted woman with dyed blonde hair coiffed in the most disciplined of waves. Uncle Allen had fallen on his feet when he met her.

My grandmother didn't approve of their union and dropped the occasional disparaging remark about *older women* and *cradle snatchers*. Once, after Aunty had left the room complaining of a hot flush, Grandma muttered, 'Hot flush my eye! She's well past hot flushes!'

I heard Dad whisper to Mum, 'Notice she says nothing about *toy boys*.'

Aunty Una was very wealthy in our eyes. Her house was vast and luxurious. She had hot and cold tap water, thick carpets, big soft armchairs *and* a piano. She also had a housekeeper, Mary. Mary cleaned the house and washed, starched and ironed Auntie's uniforms and all the linen to board-like stiffness. I slept still and rigid in the bed when I stayed there, not daring to move because the cold sheets crackled so loudly.

My Uncle Allen convinced Aunty Una to buy him a big white 1954 Plymouth Belvedere. It had soft white leather seats, white leather steering wheel and dash. They often took the whole family for a drive, as we had no car. I always sat in the front between Uncle and Aunty, and I remember one terrible day when they had a fight and started hitting each other as we drove along.

I copped quite a few of the hits until Grandma roared at them from the back seat, 'Stop that, you two! Have your fights in private.'

The rest of the journey home proceeded in tight-lipped silence.

That marriage was a volatile affair. Uncle Allen liked a drink and had an eye for other women. As well as the car, Aunty got him a boat and a holiday house at Toukley on the Central Coast. I also remember his flash gold watch and clothes. However, the relationship eventually broke up.

'Silly bugger,' said Dad when he heard.

I reflect on the black and white photos I took with the old Brownie Box, most of them copied and shared with the family over the years. They are images of times when things moved a lot more slowly – so different to this age of digital shots and phone 'selfies' which can be instantly shared on social media around the world.

I look through the viewfinder. Like me, it's speckled with age. I push the button on the side, *Click-clack.*

God bless you, Aunty Una.

She Died With Her Teeth In

It is the first house in a row of five narrow two-storey brick terraces, with common sidewalls and cast-iron balconies on the verandas upstairs. I stand at the gate, the same wire mesh gate I closed when I left there at eighteen. But that was many years ago…

We have travelled from Canberra to Sydney today, as my husband needs to see a medical specialist. We are both anxious about this visit. He is being both stoic and stubborn and does not want me with him, and so I drop him at the doctor's office and drive to a neighbouring suburb to visit the house where I spent all of my childhood.

The sign on the gate informs me that it is now a drop-in centre for the unemployed. I walk the short path to the tiny porch, glancing to the end where Grandma's chair always sat. Once, I got four small pots of enamel paint and painted the chair's wooden slats in alternate primary colours. Grandma smiled and sat down – queen of the house on her rainbow throne! She loved to sit there and nab passers-by for a chat. Later, she would hobble into the house and distribute the crumbs of gossip, sometimes sprinkled with some added spice of her own. On warm evenings, I sat on the cool tiles next to her, both of us silent. Heavy bodies languid with heat; senses saturated with sweet summer smells; listening to the hum of crickets and cicadas; watching for shooting stars.

AIR-CONDITIONED. Please Enter. I push open the front door and pass down the narrow hall. A counter blocks the entrance to what was the original front parlour of the house. That room became Grandma's bedroom because she was unable to climb the stairs.

A young woman with bright red spiky hair and many metal studs both in and on her body gets up from her desk and comes to the counter. 'Can I help you?'

'Yes, I lived here as a child and wondered if you'd mind if I had a look through?'

She stares at me and chews her bottom lip. Her hand moves towards her face and for several horrifying seconds, I think she's going to pick her nose. Instead, she merely adjusts the stud in her nostril. 'Well... yeah, sure. But there's a meeting upstairs. You can't go upstairs.' She waves her leather and metal studded wrist at me, 'Help yourself!'

'This was my grandmother's bedroom,' I say tentatively.

She gives me a *Whatever!* look and goes back to her desk.

Grandma's room. The priest came every Friday to hear her confession and administer communion. The big comfy bed, her crocheted quilt, doilies, knick-knacks, the holy pictures on the walls, hand-hooked rugs on the floor, a mirrored wardrobe and the dressing table with its treasure chest of a top drawer. Now there are filing cabinets, desks, computers, printers, and a photocopier. The aroma of Spiky's fresh cappuccino replaces the perfume of Grandma's rose-scented talc.

Grandma was very liberal with the rose-scented talc. 'Can't stand the smell of old people!' she would mutter. She was also vigilant with the tweezers. 'When you get old,' she advised, 'make sure you don't let any hair grow on your chin. I hate old ladies with whiskers!' She was quite vain. I remember the expression of horror on her face when I once walked in on her as she cleaned her false teeth. She hastily shoved them back in and told me a story of when her aunt was dying. 'They'd taken her teeth out. It was dreadful. The poor old thing had no dignity. That won't happen to me!'

She was generous with advice to all, in particular to my poor patient mother. As Grandma toddled off for her daily nap, I would hear her say to Mum, 'A short nap every afternoon adds years to your life, Betty.'

Mum would just smile; she was too busy taking care of a big family and a crippled old woman to have time for naps. I also suspect that living with Grandma had *already* added years to Mum's relatively young life.

Moving on to the living room, I encounter a swirling fog of memories. My hand grasps the stair bannister for support. My legs seem a little shaky. I am overwhelmed by my surroundings and the familiarity of that curved wooden bannister in my hand.

As I crouched in the shadows at the top of the stairs, I would clench those bannisters with both fists, straining forward to eavesdrop on the antics of the adults below.

'*If you're Irish, come into the parlour…*' I remember my father and our Irish neighbour, beers in hand, singing and swaying together. Our living room was always full of people. Aunts, uncles and cousins visiting Grandma; neighbours dropping in for a cup of tea or a few beers and a singsong on Friday or Saturday nights; Dad's mates or family gathered around our big dining table, playing cards.

A boy with dreadlocks stares at a computer in the corner where our big console wireless once had pride of place. I'd sit on the brown linoleum floor and listen with Grandma to the daytime radio serials: *Blue Hills, Ada and Elsie* or *When a Girl Marries*. Late afternoon, I would tune into *The Argonauts Club* and then the adventures of *Tarzan, Superman* or *Biggles*. On Sunday night, we would cluster round for *The Lux Radio Theatre*. Mum's hands were always busy, darning, mending or knitting; but the rest of us were still, leaning forward, our imaginations transported to a world away.

A coal fire warmed us in the winter months. Above the mantel of the fireplace was the big photograph of my grandfather and his horse Stanmore that won the Carrington Stakes. This was a bitter reminder to Grandma of more affluent times when they lived on a comfortable country property in western New South Wales. Just how bitter, I learned as an adult, when one of my aunts told me that Grandad took his mistress to Sydney to the Carrington Stakes race. Grandma found out years later and discovered that the mistress had received the gold bracelet that was part of the prize. Grandad eventually squandered the prize money of seven hundred gold sovereigns.

Occasionally, when we were short of coal, we would pinch a bit from the back of the police station up the street.

One day, as my young brother Jack was loading some coal into a hessian bag, a burly policeman strode up behind him. 'Where do you think you're going with that?'

'My Grandma's cold,' answered Jack.

'Go on then. But only this time.'

Today, the trappings of bureaucracy fill the room where once so much happened – and one dreadlocked boy replaces all the ghosts of my past.

My foot touches the familiar worn patch in the middle of the stone step between the living room and kitchen. Two girls are washing coffee cups and giggling at the sink. But I see a vision of my mother there as well – a portrait of domesticity. She looks at me with a smile as she stands at the kitchen table holding a wooden spoon, beating butter, sugar, and vanilla essence in the big cream porcelain bowl. Milk in a glass bottle, a bowl of eggs, a bag of Mothers' Choice self-raising flour, and the cake tin lined with used butter wrappings complete the scene.

I head out the back door and down the narrow path. The dilapidated, open, outside laundry where Mum stoked the fire under the copper every Monday is now a toilet block. The old separate toilet gone. I glance to where the arms of two drunken posts once juggled lines of washing until Mum steadied the whole flying circus with the wooden clothes-props.

Neat paving has now replaced the original bare dirt yard, and four young people sit smoking around an outdoor table. A serious-looking older man clasps a clipboard to his chest and talks earnestly at them. He glances up at me and I scuttle into the toilet.

The women always went in groups to the backyard lavatory. I would endeavour to be inconspicuous as I joined this gaggle of gossip and gaiety, fascinated with both the conversation and the bladder capacity of my older female relatives. I loved to play a childish game. While waiting outside the toilet, I would count out the seconds as each one peed on and on and on! Aunty Madge always won. I imagined she must have saved it up all day. However, now I think the people outside could be wondering why I am taking so long, so I head out and back up the path.

My hand reaches out to touch the sidewall as I head towards the back door. The warm, rough bricks fairly crackle with memories. Images pulse through my veins and send my head whirling, causing me to trip on the living room step. I am relieved I cannot go upstairs to revisit the three bedrooms and bathroom. I've had enough.

'Thank you,' I call to Spiky in the front room. She waves a studded wrist at me.

I recall Grandma's shaking wrist as she poured herself a tot of rum. Etched in my mind forever are the acrid smell, the glass, the rum and Grandma falling to the ground. I remember my sixteen-year-old legs sprinting the block to the public phone box. Fingers fumbling through the phonebook, unable to find the number of the Catholic presbytery to call the priest to come and give her the last rites. My whole body racked with grief, knowing I was too late.

My seventy-year-old legs are leaden as I go and pick up my husband.

He looks at me keenly. 'Are you OK?'

'I feel a bit spun out after visiting the old house! But, hey, I'm supposed to be asking you that question. What did the specialist say?'

The Day Dad Fixed the Shed

Mum was watching *Midday with Ray Martin* when I called in that day. Since her retirement, *Midday* was Mum's daytime television indulgence. We all knew better than to phone her between noon and one thirty p.m. She wouldn't answer the phone or would dismiss the caller with a quick 'I'll phone you back. Ray's on.'

I sat and watched the last five minutes of the show with her. There was no point in trying to make conversation, she was getting a bit deaf lately, and the television volume was very loud.

'Where's Dad?' I asked as the show ended.

'He's fixing the shed roof. It leaked yesterday in that heavy rain.' She looked at her watch as she switched off the TV. 'He's been up there for ages. It must be a big job.'

Just then, I heard a yell from the backyard. I raced out and could see the top half of Dad sticking out of the roof of the old shed. 'What happened?'

'What does it bloody look like? I fell through and I'm stuck. I've been calling out to your mother for hours. A man could've bloody died up here! Alone!'

Mum was there by then and I heard her give a little splutter of laughter. I looked in the shed door at Dad's dangling feet. He'd been supporting himself on his elbows, and the weight of his body on the roof must have jammed him in.

'Dad, we'll get something solid under your feet first and make you more comfortable before we decide what to do.'

'We should call the fire brigade,' suggested Mum.

'I don't want the bloody fire brigade,' said Dad.

I made a stack from a milk crate, an old wooden box, and a few bricks and guided Dad's feet onto that.

'Call Joe Brady and see if he's home,' said Dad. 'He'll know what to do.'

Mrs Strickland's face appeared over the back fence. 'Hello, Jack,' she said with a smug grin. 'In a bit of a tight spot?'

Dad and Mrs Strickland had been enemies for thirty years, ever since she lopped off his choko vine and threw it back over the fence. The primary vine on our side soon died, and Dad swore she'd poisoned it. He called her Mrs Strychnine and said he wished he could give her a dose of her own medicine. 'Poisonous old busybody.'

Joe Brady arrived and gave a long, low whistle when he saw Dad's problem. 'I'll go and see Bob. He's got an angle grinder.'

While we were waiting, Mrs Strickland suggested that as the old shed was leaning sideways anyway, we could just push it down. Dad and his mates had cobbled the shed together from bits and pieces when we first moved into the house. It had always looked a bit discombobulated, and we were all surprised that it had stayed standing all these years. Dad knew that Mrs Strickland hated it as it spoiled the view from her kitchen into our yard.

'Yeah, great,' said Dad. 'Push the shed down and cut me bloody in half.'

'Can I get you a cup of tea, Jack?' asked Mum.

'I just want to get out of here. I don't need cups of tea.'

'I still think we should call the fire brigade,' said Mum.

'Why don't you call Channel 7 and the bloody helicopter as well!' exploded Dad.

Jill Jenkins arrived home next door with her two preschoolers and came in to see if she could help. Their yappy dog came with them, ran into the shed and got very excited by Dad's teetering legs. Next, we heard a loud yelp from the dog and a sharp 'Bloody hell!' from Dad. It took us ages to restack the milk crate, the box and bricks under Dad's feet. Jenny said the dog was okay.

Joe and Bob came back with various tools.

'We can't cut around you, Jack,' said Bob. 'You're jammed in too tight. We'll start from the edge if we can and work across.' However, as they started to prise up the edge of the roof, Bob stopped. 'You know, Jack, I don't think this'll work. The whole shed might come down.'

'And cut him in half,' smiled Mrs Strickland.

'I'm calling the fire brigade,' said Mum.

'Good idea,' said Joe.

Marion Henshaw arrived home from her shift at the hospital, saw the mob in the yard, and came over. She'd saved Dad's life last year when he had his heart attack, giving him CPR for fifteen minutes until the ambulance arrived to whisk him off for his triple bypass.

'How's your blood pressure now, Jack?' she asked.

'Under control,' said Mum. 'Well, mostly…'

'How long's he been there?'

'Bloody hours,' said Dad.

Marion went and phoned for an ambulance. Just in case.

The fire brigade must have been having a quiet afternoon, as four firefighters now clumped into the yard in their big boots. I noticed a couple of them trying to suppress a smile when they saw Dad's predicament. They surveyed the scene, and I heard one say, 'Jaws of life.'

'Strewth,' sighed Dad.

Kids in the street arriving home from school spotted the fire engine. The word spread. Children and mothers filed into the yard to see what was going on. Neighbours who hadn't spoken for years caught up with each other's news.

Poor Dad stood there amidst the chatter and laughter, alone in his misery.

A loud cheer rose from the many onlookers as he was finally released. The paramedics wanted to take him to the hospital, but Dad refused.

They sat him down and checked his blood pressure. 'A bit high, but not bad given the circumstances.'

Surprisingly, the shed continued to stand – still with its drunken lean and now minus half a roof.

'I'll come back tomorrow and help you fix that roof, Jack,' said Joe Brady.

'Thanks, Joe,' Dad nodded, giving Mrs Strickland a smug look.

The firefighters let all the younger children take turns to sit in the fire engine. We heard the loud wail of the siren as it went, a mob of yelling kids chasing it down the street.

Mum told Dad to sit in the lounge room while she made a nice cup of tea.

'A man could've died up there!' muttered Dad, collapsing dramatically into his chair.

I heard a splutter of laughter from the kitchen.

The Funeral

Driving the Hume Highway from Canberra to Sydney, I noticed the speedometer hit a hundred and thirty kilometres an hour. I unclenched my hands from the steering wheel, took a deep breath, and eased my foot off the accelerator. I wondered how Mum would react when she heard the news…

The family gathered from near and far in our parents' home.

'We'll have to go to the hospital and tell Mum…' The anguish in Mary's voice reflected the despair we all felt.

I was the eldest. I stood up. 'Come on then, I'll do it.'

I was shocked when I saw my mother sitting on the hard chair in the hospital room. She was always so particular about her appearance, but now her hair was uncombed and her dress grubby. Worst of all, her eyes were dead.

I took her hand, looked into those vacant eyes, and told her that Dad had died suddenly that morning.

'What happened?' she asked.

'Cathy called into the house and found him, Mum.'

My heart was breaking. My poor sister Cathy and the horror she must have faced that morning. My poor Mum alone here in this dreadful hospital room. The shock now confronting the whole family.

Mum made a terrible little mewing noise. 'I should have been there,' she said.

Our lovely, laughing mother – the rock of our family. We were all so reliant on her unfailing presence that we failed to notice her slipping away, descending silently into a deep, unfathomable pit of depression until finally two weeks ago, in terrible, unimaginable despair, she had slashed her wrists.

The hospital staff agreed that Mum could return home for the funeral, providing someone was with her at all times. We made a sorry procession as we approached the empty house. She went straight to her bedroom and crawled into bed fully clothed without a word.

My sisters and brothers returned to their respective homes, leaving me to stay with Mum. I collected all the sharp kitchen knives and scissors and hid them in my room. I spent a sleepless night, grieving for my beloved father and listening out for any movement from a mother who was also lost.

Next morning, Mum refused to get out of bed. 'I can't go to the funeral.'

'Mum, the funeral is two days away. Why can't you go?'

She looked confused for a second and then said, 'My hair's a mess.'

'I'll set it for you.'

'Setting's no good. It needs a perm.'

'Okay. I'll take you to the hairdressers.'

'No. I can't face the hairdressers.'

I drove to the shopping centre and purchased a home permanent wave kit. I managed to get her out of bed and seated at the kitchen table while I tried to decipher the instructions on the box. *It couldn't be that hard!*

She grumbled and whined as I struggled with recalcitrant plastic perm rods and foul-smelling lotion. Our loving mother who never complained – who had never uttered an unkind word to me before in her life. This terrible mental illness had created a monster.

Perm complete and hair set in rollers, she went back to bed. A short time later, I passed the door to see the rollers out and strewn across the bedroom floor – Mum's thin body curled in a foetal position on the doona.

On the morning of the funeral, she informed us that she wasn't going.

'Don't worry, Jude, I'll talk her around,' said my youngest brother, Jack.

Jack had a silver tongue and could always talk Mum around. I left him to it.

Five minutes later, he came out to the kitchen. 'She's adamant she's not going.'

I rushed back into the bedroom, slapping away the tears that suddenly appeared on my cheeks. 'Mum, if you don't get out of that bed right now, I'll have to stay here and look after you. That means I won't be able to go to my own father's funeral. Mum, that's just not fair!'

She gave me a sheepish look and got out of bed.

'Let me do your hair, Mum.'

She stood sullen and forlorn in front of the bathroom mirror as I brushed and fluffed up the curls. The smell of the permanent wave lotion was still quite strong. I wondered if perhaps I hadn't rinsed it enough. I grabbed the can of spray from the bathroom cabinet and liberally sprayed her hair.

'What are you doing? Now I *know* you're trying to kill me!'

I looked at the spray can in my hand. It was fly spray! *What was that doing in the bathroom?* Previously, something like this would have sent my mother into hoots of laughter. *But not this Mum!*

I found the hairspray, but she was having none of it.

'Just leave me alone! You've done enough damage.' She stalked off to the bedroom and lay down, rubbing her head back and forth against the pillow.

As my sister Mary left the house on the evening of Dad's death, she said, 'I've spoken to Father Matthew. He might call in and see you. Just be prepared – he's Indian and has very black skin.'

'What?''I cried. 'We can't have him!'

'What do you mean?'

'We can't have a black, Indian priest for Dad's funeral. You know what Dad was like!' We all knew that Dad's views on *bloody foreigners* made Pauline Hanson look like Mother Teresa.

'I fought in a war to stop Australia being invaded,' I heard Dad say once, 'but it's happened anyway.' And no amount of rational argument about the benefits of multiculturalism could convince him to change his mind.

'Father Matthew is very nice,' Mary called back over her shoulder as she went down the front steps. 'He'll be fine.'

Father Matthew was very nice. I met him eventually in the car park at the cemetery just before the funeral. He was very tall and very black. I couldn't decide if his deep, melodic voice reminded me of Kamahl or Peter Sellers. *Goodness gracious me,* I thought.

I had written a few lines about my father's life and asked Father Matthew if he would include them in the service.

'Wouldn't someone in the family like to read this, Judy?'

I shook my head. The shock of Dad's death and Mum's illness had left us all just too shattered.

On my sheet, I had included particulars of Dad's family: his wife Betty, his three daughters, two sons, nineteen grandchildren and two great-grandchildren.

Well, Father Matthew must have been impressed with Jack Townsend's contribution to the Catholic population and started every sentence with full details of 'Brother Jack's' family. I felt my brother Michael flinch the first time we heard it. We turned simultaneously towards the coffin, almost expecting Dad to sit up and cry, 'I'm not your bloody brother, mate!'

However, Father Matthew's rich, lilting Indian accent rolled on, dipping and rising, making me feel a bit seasick. 'Our brother Jack will be sadly missed by his wife Betty, his three daughters, two sons, nineteen grandchildren and two great-grandchildren.'

He went on and on, sentence after sentence concluded with the total impressive numbers of *Brother Jack's family.* I could now feel Michael shaking and wondered, *was it with horror or silent laughter?* Lips pressed together; I dipped my head. I didn't dare look at Michael. Mum sat on my left; chin slumped on her chest; eyes closed. *Oh, it was all too bizarre, terrible and hysterical!*

Later, at the wake in the back garden, Mum amazed us all by playing the perfect host to all the relatives and well-wishers who came. However, as soon as they left, she took herself off to bed, leaving just the immediate family to reflect on the day.

Young Jack lightened the mood when he did an impersonation of Father Matthew's *Brother Jack* routine. I guess it was a bit irreverent, but we agreed that, for all Dad's xenophobia and bigotry, he *did* have a great sense of humour and would definitely have seen the irony of it all!

The full impact of my father's death didn't really hit me until two months later. I caught the train from Canberra to Sydney to visit Mum. As I walked down the railway ramp, I found myself looking out for Dad. He often met me. The shock of him not being there was heart-rending. I sat on the seat in the little park by the station. The pansies were putting on a riotous show. *Dad would have loved them.* Rising slowly, I set out on the walk up the hill to the house.

I gave a tentative knock on the front door, remembering the terrible times of my last visit. Mum opened the door. She was wearing navy slacks, a crisp white blouse; a red cardigan with a gold brooch pinned to one side and her hair was freshly washed and set. Best of all, her eyes were smiling. *My mother was back.*

Watermelon Days

As we walked along the dirt road, my eyes were level with the back of my father's left hand. He had an interesting hand. It was brown and strong with a deep scar in the middle. Black hairs spilt from under the leather strap of his watchband and trickled down around the scar and thinned out at the base of his fingers.

'How did you get that scar, Dad?' I asked.

'In the war,' he answered, and somehow, I knew not to ask any more.

Clouds of locusts rose from the parched grass on the side of the road as we walked. I kicked the road's talcum-like dust, enjoying the spray of fine clouds around us. Mum would have told me to stop and chastised me for ruining my new sandals. Dad took my small hand in his and led me onto the dry grassy verge. He encouraged me to stomp and crunch on the locusts.

I loved our summer holidays in the country with my grandparents. It was January 1950, and we had arrived the day before, travelling overnight by steam train from Sydney.

The country rail section of Central Station was a chaos of activity, noise, people and steam. Dad struggled with the 'ports' as we called the suitcases in those days. Mum directed me to keep close as she juggled the baby, string bags of food and stuff for the trip while we pushed our way through the crowds on the platform.

The enormous steam engine hissed impatiently as we scrambled on board, found our reserved seats and spread ourselves around in the compartment. I bounced on the firm leather of the long bench seat and watched Dad heave the luggage up onto the wrought-iron racks. Mum collapsed on the bench opposite me with a sigh of relief. I took in my surroundings: the black and white photos of scenes of rail destinations in New South Wales and the carafe of water with two glasses in a holder on the wall. Each of the two benches in the compartment seated four, and we hoped that no one else would join us so we could stretch out a little to sleep.

Dad encouraged me to be a bit raucous if anyone approached and he would wink at Mum and say, 'Better pinch the baby, Bette, and make her cry.'

We woke the next morning as the train pulled into Werris Creek for refreshments. No toast tasted as good as that Werris Creek refreshment room toast! Then the onwards journey towards Manilla. I hung out the window, waiting to spot the huge wheat silos that heralded our destination.

'You'll get soot in your eyes,' Mum warned. She pulled out a wet washer and vigorously scrubbed my face just before the train pulled in.

Grandfather waited at the station with his horse and cart and we clip-clopped through the town, across the bridge and down the road to the old country house to find my grandmother waiting, shading her wrinkled eyes with one hand. She ushered us into the kitchen for tea, Sao biscuits with cheese and sliced tomato, and scones with jam and cream.

On this second day of our holiday, Dad and I were despatched to Billy Sing's market garden to buy a watermelon. Rows and rows of vegetables and melons soon came into view. Billy and his family bent in the fields in the burning afternoon sun, tending and nurturing with a calm and patient rhythm.

A metal triangle hung from a rope attached to the ceiling of the back veranda of the house. Next to that dangled another rope with a straight piece of iron.

My father lifted me up. 'Only hit it three times. That'll be enough.'

Clang, clang, clang, echoed out over the fields. The gardeners looked up. Billy Sing straightened his back and came slowly through a long row of plump green lettuce towards us.

G'days exchanged, I shuffled my feet while the two men went through the ritual small talk.

'Locusts givin' you any trouble, Billy?'

'Nah! Seen worse than this.'

'Enough rain this season?'

'Nah! But we pump from the river. It's still runnin'.'

Dad glanced towards the benches and wooden boxes of produce lined neatly along the wall of the veranda. 'After a watermelon for the kids today, Billy.'

Billy strolled over to four lovely plump green melons lying side by side like fat little elongated Buddhas. He tapped each one with his knuckle. Dad followed him. He also tapped, both men listening seriously to the hollow *frump, frump.*

'This one,' said Billy.

Dad gave it another rap and nodded. Next came the part that always thrilled me. It was the ultimate test! Billy picked up his big sharp carving knife, cut a neat triangle of skin, and magically lifted out, like a jewel from the Buddha's forehead, a beautiful, perfect, triangular plug of juicy red flesh for us to inspect.

'Good one,' said Billy.

'Yeah,' said Dad. 'She'll do.'

Billy replaced the plug neatly back into the melon. I always begged to eat this special piece when we got home. To me, it seemed the most delicious and magical part of the whole fruit. Billy weighed the melon on the old scales, payment made, and we set off back up the dusty road with our prize.

My grandmother spread newspaper on the cobblestones under the vine-covered pergola that lay between the kitchen and main part of the house. We settled in the cool of the vines – adults and kids – juice dripping from our chins and down our arms as we ate the delicious red flesh and spat the seeds out onto the paper.

'You should save these seeds and grow some, Col,' my father said to my grandfather.

Grandfather's summer garden had an abundance of squash, marrow, tomatoes and miscellaneous vegetables, but never melons.

'No,' replied my grandfather quietly. 'No one grows watermelons like Billy Sing.'

When I decided to write this story, I contacted the historian at the Manilla Heritage Museum to seek help with research on the Sing family and the history of market gardens in the area. I made an astonishing discovery that stirred up more memories of my father:

Dad, Mum, and I were at the War Memorial in Canberra in the late 1970s, inspecting the remains of a Japanese submarine that invaded Sydney Harbour during the Second World War.

'I don't know how they could've possibly coped with being under-water in that confined space,' said my mother with a shudder.

'The mongrels weren't human,' muttered Dad.

At the same time, I spotted a group of Japanese tourists, cameras in hand, heading our way. Dad saw them too and visibly blanched. He stood stock-still, stared at them for a few seconds and then hurried off. The afternoon was a complete failure after that. Dad didn't want to look at any of the exhibits. He never spoke of his war experiences in New Guinea but made it clear that he hated the Japanese.

A fact reinforced a few years later, while Mum and Dad were again visiting and my small son brought home a Japanese friend to play after school. I thought nothing of it until Dad got up and headed out the door.

I chased him up the street. 'Dad, I'm sorry if that little Japanese boy upset you. Dad, he's only six years old. He had nothing to do with the war.'

My father looked down at the back of his trembling hand and shook his head. 'I'll just go for a walk.'

The historian at the Manilla Heritage Museum revealed to me that the original Sing who established the market gardens in the area in the late 1800s, was, in fact, Japanese.

My mother was astounded when I told her. She and her parents (and I suspect all the people in the town) always thought the Sings were Chinese.

'Old Sam Sing and Billy Sing were both lovely, decent men,' said Mum. 'Billy was always very kind to you children. Your father always liked him.'

I agreed, thinking back on the times Dad and Billy stood together, comfortably yarning on the back veranda of Billy's house.

Last night, as I watched hideous scenes of war, hate, death and disease on the television news, I remembered Billy Sing placing the watermelon in Dad's outstretched hands…

My father was a gentle, decent man, fiercely loyal to his family and friends. I find it difficult to reconcile his flashes of xenophobia and bigotry with the man who laughed with his children and grandchildren and tended his flower garden with such tender care.

I wonder to this day what atrocities Dad witnessed to hate the Japanese so. However, I am pleased that my father died before he knew Billy was not Chinese. We might never have experienced those wonderful Watermelon Days.

www.ingramcontent.com/pod-product-compliance
Lightning Source LLC
Chambersburg PA
CBHW051234210726
48290CB00003B/947